BOUND TO EXECUTE

ST. MARIN'S COZY MYSTERY 3

ACF BOOKENS

1

I have this not-yet-explored fascination with garden magazines. Every time I see one and have the cash on hand, I pick it up. I'm such a sucker for those images of great planters and perfect levels of colorful flowers that I have to limit myself to cash-only purchases lest I spend my mortgage money on magazines that I don't have any time to read.

So why I thought I'd start not one but two gardens while also running my own bookstore, I don't know. But I did . . . and I was loving it. At home, my roommate and best friend, Mart, and I had built some raised beds from fence boards that were left behind when we bought the house, and at the shop, I gathered a variety of planters from yard sales and auctions – with the help of my friends Stephen and Walter, denizens of good bargains and great taste – to arrange in front of the bookstore.

At home, the planting was easy. We put in vegetable starts from our friend Elle Heron's farm stand – tomatoes and peppers and one eggplant because I had this vision of suddenly liking the vegetable if I grew it. Plus, we seeded some carrots, beans, and melons, and I got very excited by the prospect of harvesting and then cooking with the food fresh from the yard. I was very optimistic.

The bookstore plants proved more daunting because I wanted to recreate, so very badly, those gorgeous photos from the books. Elle cautioned me, though, about the various light and water needs of the eighty-eight flowers or so that I had dog-eared in the gardening magazines and suggested I go simple. Thus, I stuck with calibrachoa in a beautiful butter yellow and magenta coleus to complement it. I loved the look of those colors, even though – as several enthusiastic (and several other slightly angry) customers pointed out – I had inadvertently given tribute to the Redskins football team. Ravens' fans were angry that I hadn't, apparently, genetically altered flowers to make them teal and black, but I didn't point out that I was a bookseller, not a horti-culturist. I also didn't say that I would never support – with my flowers or my money – the Redskins, given their racist mascot and team name. I wasn't always good at holding my tongue, but in this case, I did. No need to make customers angry, after all.

Still, the pots – alongside the bench my friend Woody had made – gave the converted gas station a welcoming feel. Customers often sat out there with a cup of coffee from Rocky's café and enjoyed the spring weather. The first two weeks of May on the Eastern Shore are picture perfect for sitting and basking in the spring sun. Temperatures in the seventies. A slight breeze off the water. Perfect.

In fact, most days when my assistant manager, Marcus, came in, I took my place on that bench for that very reason. Mayhem, my Black Mouth Cur, had figured out that the sun hit the west side of that bench perfectly in the afternoon, so she never hesitated to bed down in a sunbeam while I turned my face toward the sky and soaked in some Vitamin D.

It was in that face-up position that Henri Johnson found me on that early May afternoon. "Hi Harvey," she said as she dropped onto the bench next to me.

I sat up just a little to turn toward her, but quickly resumed my position when she, too, leaned back, closed her eyes, and sighed. "What brings you by, Henri? Need some more books?"

"Not yet, my dear. Bear brought me the last orders, and I'm still working through them. Just hard to stay inside and read when the weather is this nice."

I patted the copy of *Crime and Punishment* next to me. "That's why I always bring a book."

She laughed. "I see how much reading you're getting done at the moment."

I peeked over at my friend and marveled at the beautiful pink tones under her brown skin. Henri had the best complexion of anyone I knew, by far. I'd asked her once what she used, and she'd held up a pile of wool roving from next to her spinning wheel. "Lanolin. All natural."

Henri was a weaver – a really good one. One of her pieces was the runner for our dining table at home, but just this week, Mart and I had talked about asking her to make us a new piece for the table, something lighter for summer.

We sat quietly for several minutes as the sun warmed us. I relished these days before humidity. I had grown up just north of here, and I knew a Maryland summer was not something to be trifled with, especially if you had curly hair like I did. Humidity and curls are not a good combination. But these perfectly warm days, I could do with months of those.

Eventually, though, I felt the tell-tale tingle of a sunburn coming on and thought it best to put on my ball cap and begin the walk home. As I sat forward, Henri stood, too. "Thanks for that moment of rest, Harvey. I saw you here on my way to the bank and just couldn't resist."

"Well, Henri, I'm honored to have had your company on the bench to bask. Let's do it again before the town becomes a sauna."

"Deal." She gave my arm a pat before she headed on up the street, a blue bank envelope in her hand.

Seeing her deposit envelope made me glance at my watch – 4:45 – just enough time to get an extra deposit in before the weekend. I bustled inside and headed for the register. Marcus was just ringing up a sale, so I gave him a wink as I settled onto the stool behind him to wait.

As always, he had hand-sold the customer some of his favorite books. Right now, he was on a Louise Erdrich kick, and I saw that the woman was leaving with copies of both *The Round House* and her new book, *The Night Watchman*. The woman was smiling, and I knew Marcus had secured another customer for the store. For about the millionth time I thought how lucky I was to have met him and to have been able to convince him to work with me.

He smiled at me. "Whatcha need, Ms. B? Forget something?"

"Nope. Just decided to do an extra deposit before the weekend. Feeling flush with our big sales this week." I laughed. It hadn't exactly been a big enough week that I could afford a yacht like some of those now coming into the St. Marin's marina for the season, but each week, we were selling a bit more, and I hoped by our one-year anniversary in the fall we'd be ready to bring on a third employee.

"Sounds good." He leaned down, unlocked the cabinet door, and then opened the small safe we kept there. "Always good to keep your cash in the bank, Mama says. Less likely to spend it that way."

Marcus's mom, Josie, was a regular columnist in our monthly newsletter. Her book reviews were almost as good as her son's, and I loved her humor and the wisdom it usually hid within.

"Well, if Josie says it's wise, then it must be doubly so." I patted Marcus on his shoulder blade. "You been working out, Marcus? Seems like you might be beefing up a bit."

A flash of color ran up under Marcus's walnut skin. "Maybe a little." His eyes darted over to the café behind me, and I smiled.

"Ah, I see. Well, it looks good on you." Marcus and café owner Rocky had been dating for a few weeks now, and from the pep in their steps and Marcus's newly acquired interest in weight-lifting, it seemed like things were going well.

I slid the cash and checks into our red bank envelope and made a note of what was there before heading to the door. "See you tomorrow." I waved at Marcus and went out below the dinging bell.

Mayhem's sunbeam had moved on, so she was ready to walk. I slid her leash out of the custom-made holder that Woody had added to the bench when he'd realized how much Mayhem loved laying by it and headed in Henri's footsteps to the bank.

It was just a few doors down Main Street to the bank, but it was 4:55 now – and banks didn't make a habit of staying open a minute late, especially not ours. The bank manager, Wilma Painter, was a fastidious, rule-following woman, and none of the business owners in town trifled with her if we could help it. She'd been known to literally slam the bank door on a customer's hand if they dared to try and open it a minute past five.

A woman in her fifties, she had apparently decided to fight the signs of aging with coal-black hair-dye, and unfortunately, Wilma was a woman prone to glistening, as my mother delicately called sweating. So on a warm day, or when things in the bank went a little awry of Wilma's strict standards, rivulets of black stain ran down her cheekbones. I always felt a little bad for her, but I didn't know how – or have the courage – to suggest a visit to a professional salon lest my accounts be closed immediately.

I bustled into the bank lobby at 4:56 and breathed a sigh of relief to see no one ahead of me in line. Some businesses have the, "If you're in the door before closing" policy, but not Wilma's bank. She would march you right out the door at five p.m. if your transaction wasn't finished. I had found that out the hard way one day when she'd grabbed my arm, not gently, and walked me out the door, shutting it snugly after she said, "We reopen on Monday at nine a.m."

The teller gave me a tight smile as I approached. "Hi Cynthia. Sorry to be cutting it so close."

The young woman, who was a frequent visitor to my bookstore's romance section, said, "It's okay. I can count fast," and then proceeded to count my deposit with the lightning speed that the three minutes left in her work day required. She printed the slip just as the clock over her head read 4:59, and I turned to go. But just then, I heard shouting from the direction of Wilma's office.

I turned to see what the commotion was about just as Henri came storming out of the office. Wilma followed behind her, her voice even but steely. "Ms. Johnson, I'll appreciate that you speak to me with respect. This is a place of business."

Henri turned, opened her mouth as if to say something, and then spun back around and walked out of the building.

I stood, dumbfounded, in the middle of the lobby until Wilma spotted me. "Ms. Beckett, please close your mouth and leave. It is 5:02 p.m.," she said as she checked her watch, "and you are now in violation of bank policy. Remain any longer, and I will have to call the police and ask that you be removed."

I lowered my chin and looked at the bank manager from under my eyebrows, but I knew there was no value in giving her a piece of my mind, even if I did relish the idea of Sheriff Mason having to come escort me out for being in the bank at 5:02 p.m. The sheriff and I were good friends, and I knew for a fact that he harbored no deep affection for Wilma Painter. Still, I wasn't in the mood to ruin my Friday night with a stand-off, so I turned, thanked Cynthia again, and went out the door.

Mayhem was waiting by the tree to which I'd tied her, but she was turned back up the street and pulling at her leash. I looked in the direction she was straining and saw Henri leaning up against the wall of the bookstore. Her shoulders were heaving.

I gathered Mayhem and quickly headed that way. "Henri, are you okay? Do you want to come inside and sit down?"

When she lifted her head I saw, though, that she wasn't crying. No, this woman was furious, and she was taking long, hard breaths to, it seemed, calm down. "I'm sorry, Harvey, but that woman."

I nodded. "She is something. Just threatened to have Tuck come and escort me out."

Henri shook her head. "She is really unbelievable." She took a hard breath and dropped her shoulders. "I wouldn't want this getting around town, but she just threatened to foreclose on the co-op."

"What?!" The art co-op down the street was one of the biggest attractions in St. Marin's. Henri had a studio there, and so did our friend Cate, a local photographer known for her portraits. "Why?"

Henri gritted her teeth. "She says that we are behind on our mortgage payments, but that can't be right, can it? I mean, Cate is on top of everything. I can't imagine her missing a payment."

I agreed. Cate had quickly become one of my dearest friends, and she was one of the most organized, thoughtful people I knew. She would never risk putting the co-op or the artists it served at risk. "I can't imagine that either. There must be some other explanation."

Henri met my eye. "You're right. Thanks, Harvey. It's just the way Wilma talked to me, like I was an idiot."

"I know. She is ridiculous." I smiled. "We can figure this all out, though. I'm sure there's some simple story here."

She nodded, then looked at her watch. "Shoot. I'm afraid I can't figure it out now, though. Bear has one of those fancy hospital dinners, and I have to get home and get ready."

I clasped her arm, and we walked up Main Street to the co-op. "Don't worry. Cate and Lucas are coming to my place for dinner tonight. If it's okay with you, I'll tell her what happened and see what she says. Email you later with the story?"

Henri squeezed my hand on her arm. "Oh, that would be great, Harvey. Thanks." She turned to me. "And thanks for calming me down." She gave me a quick hug and then scratched Mayhem behind the ears. "Talk to you tomorrow."

"Definitely. And I'll email tonight for sure."

She hurried down the sidewalk and got into her old, green Jaguar. I waved as she pulled by and then took a deep breath. At least we'd have something to talk about at dinner.

I pulled my phone out of my back pocket. I still had a little time before I needed to go home, so I pointed my feet toward the mechanic's shop at the end of the street. That was all the signal

Mayhem needed to head toward her best friend, Taco, the Bassett Hound. I didn't blame her though. A certain handsome mechanic kind of made me want to run, too.

Daniel was under the front of a blue sedan when we arrived. I could just see his denim-clad legs sticking out. Next to him, the prostrate body of the Bassett Hound lay as if waiting to hand him the next tool . . . well, except for the floppy ear over his eye. Taco was not much good at assisting with anything except weighing down objects and nap training. Still, he was excellent company.

Mayhem wasted no time and stretched out beside him. "I brought another useless assistant for you."

"Oh, hi," Daniel said as he began to slide out on his roller-thingy. I knew that slider contraption he used to get under cars had a name, and I'd even asked, twice. But I'd forgotten both times since I had no compartments for car-related info in my brain, well, unless it related to a book. When I'd read *The Myth of Solid Ground* by David Ulin – an amazing book about earthquakes – I'd learned that James Dean died in a Porsche Spyder on the San Andreas fault, and I had never forgotten. Give me a story, and I'll remember. Otherwise, I couldn't tell an alternator from a brake caliper.

Daniel stood and eyed the two dogs beside him. "Useless, those two. Completely useless."

I stepped forward and gave him a kiss on the cheek, taking a second to breath in that scent of oil and aftershave that I'd come to love even before I'd been willing to tell the man wearing them that I felt the same about him. That hurdle in our relationship had been crossed a few weeks back, though, and now we were sliding into that phase that was about resting easy in affection but not pushing too hard for the next step. I liked this stage, secure and steady with not much pressure.

"Utterly," I said as he leaned over and kissed my cheek.

"To what do I owe the pleasure of this visit?" Daniel asked as he wiped his hands on a blue rag. The man collected rags like they were gold, and I was grateful since I'd been able to gift him all the frayed and stained hand towels at our house without guilt.

"We were just out and about with a little time to kill." I tried to sound nonchalant.

"Oh yeah. Since when do you have time to kill? I mean I appreciate the visit, but wouldn't you rather be squeezing in a chapter of your latest read before dinner?"

He had a point. Ever since the shop had gotten its feet under it and Marcus had begun working full-time, I'd delved back into my reading life with gusto. Daniel, not much of a reader himself, couldn't figure out why I had this obsession with books, but I couldn't figure out his obsession with cars, so I wagered we were even. "Well, yeah, okay. This weird thing happened with Henri at the bank."

I told him about Henri's fight with Wilma and the missing payments. "Doesn't seem like Cate to let something like that slip," he said as he heaved Taco to a standing position before starting to turn off the shop lights.

"That's what I said. She's just too organized for that."

He slipped an only slightly dirty arm around my waist as I encouraged Mayhem to standing with her leash. "You're going to ask her tonight, right?"

"Yep. Sure am. And speaking of which, I better get home and get the hamburgers formed up. I'm adding steak sauce and tucking cheese in the middle. I feel so fancy."

He grinned. "Need a hand? I mean, I'd like to shower, but I can come on if that would help."

I smiled. "You go shower. I can handle the burgers, and I have an audiobook to listen to while I cook."

"Of course you do," he said, giving me a quick kiss before I went out the door. "See you at six-thirty."

He gave a wave as he bent down to lift Taco, who had returned to his previous prone position in the ten seconds that Daniel and I were talking.

MAYHEM PULLED me home with her incessant sniffing, which apparently wore her out because when we got the house, she went right to her dog bed and collapsed. Aslan, my cat, was less than thrilled to be displaced from her makeshift bed in the sun, but the dog was not to be dissuaded. Aslan begrudgingly took up her place on the cashmere throw on my reading chair. Oh, to have the life of one of my pets.

I opened up the e-lending app for the St. Marin's library and click on Patrick Ness's *The Rest of Us Just Live Here*. I'd long been an audiobook listener, but it had taken me a while to warm to checking out audiobooks electronically from the library. I don't really know why I'd stalled – this was the best thing, even if the selection was a bit limited. I knew libraries thrived on circulation numbers, so checking out my audiobooks when I could made sense. Plus, the due date made me listen more and, thus, read more books. It was a win-win.

I had just flipped the burgers in the skillet when I heard car doors slam and the skitter of Mayhem's nails as she went to welcome everyone. In came most of the people I loved: Mart; Stephen and Walter; Cate and her husband, Lucas; my parents, Sharon and Burt; and, of course, Daniel. I glanced at the clock on the microwave – six-thirty on the dot. A punctual bunch, these.

Mart brought in four bottles of wine from the winery where

she worked, including a chardonnay that I loved. Mom and Dad brought salad as requested. Stephen and Walter came bearing some steamed green beans with dill and lemon, and Lucas and Cate carried in two bakery boxes that were, without a doubt, the best cupcakes in all the world. Lucas was the director at the maritime museum in town, but I was not the only person who said he could open a cupcake shop in a heartbeat.

The dogs – Mayhem and Taco – and their two buddies, Sidecar, Mom and Dad's rescue, and Sasquatch, Cate and Lucas's Miniature Schnauzer, went right to the water bowl before draping themselves over the cluster of dog beds in the corner of the living room. They were sleeping soundly before we even got the plates out.

This had become our new Friday night ritual, and even in just a month's worth of Friday evenings, we'd fallen into a routine. Stephen and Walter set the table while Mart and Dad got drinks. Mom helped me plate up the burgers and fixings, and Daniel fed the pups under the careful and skeptical eye of Aslan, who could not be bribed – even with tuna – to eat until she had her kitchen back to herself.

We weren't a formal crowd, so everyone grabbed mismatched plates and filled them up before taking seats on the couch and floor in the living room. We didn't have enough dining room chairs for everyone, and also, it felt cozier, more fun, to just picnic in the living room.

I forced myself to wait to ask Cate about the co-op until the second bottle of wine was open, but then my curiosity – a trait my mother had always called nosiness – got the better of me. "Cate, I ran into Henri today. She got into a real hullaballoo with Wilma over at the bank."

"She did? That doesn't seem like Henri." She took a sip of wine.

"But then again, it does seem like Wilma, so . . . what was the ruckus about?"

It was my turn to take a sip of wine. "Well, I told Henri I'd ask you about it and let her know, but apparently, Wilma said the bank is going to foreclose on the co-op because the mortgage hasn't been paid."

I put my wine glass up to my mouth and tilted it back both as shield and salve.

"What in the—?" Cate was on her feet faster than I could blink.

Lucas stood with her and put a hand on her arm. "This must be a mistake, Cate. We can clear it up first thing Monday. Or we can call Wilma at home, if we can find her number."

Cate slapped his hand away. "Of course it's a mistake. And any self-respecting banker who had been dealing with another business for as long as they have should know that there's a mistake. How dare she threaten to foreclose without talking to me! How dare she give that information to anyone but me!" Cate's voice had gotten very quiet, and I could see from the set of her jaw that the quiet belied the rage.

I let out a long breath, hoping that might inspire Cate to do the same, but instead, she locked eyes on me. "You say Wilma Painter had the gall to bring this up just before the close of business on a Friday? That woman is unbelievable. Unbelievable and cowardly. When I get my hands on her—"

"We all know this is a mistake, Cate." Daniel's voice was firm and even. "And we all have your back. We won't let Wilma do anything to the co-op." He wasn't a man of many words, but when he spoke, people listened. The energy in the room was quelled to only slightly uncomfortable.

Cate's eyes welled up. "I know. Thank you, Daniel, but it's a bank. Banks are ruthless institutions. If they think I haven't been paying our mortgage . . ." Her eyes snapped up to mine. "Oh, Harvey. How was Henri? She must have been horrified."

"Apoplectic might be a better adjective. She knew there was an error, and she was furious that Wilma would contend that it was some lack of judgment or moral diligence that caused this situation." I waited a minute and hoped there was enough oxygen in the room to handle my next question. "I told her I'd ask you about it and let her know. Do you have any idea what happened?"

My question brought Cate to her knee on the floor. Lucas handed back her wine glass, and she took a long sip. "I don't. I send the payment with the deposit on the last day of the month. Always have."

Stephen leaned forward. "You don't pay it electronically?"

Cate shook her head. "Nope. I knew I could have, and Wilma put some pressure on me to do that – I expect I'll hear a big ole hair-dye-stained 'I told you' so on that one now – but it always seemed easier to just write up the transfer form and put it in with the cash. That way, there was a paper trail."

I stared down into my now-empty wine glass. "Did you take the deposits yourself?"

Cate's eyes whipped up to mine. "No. No, I didn't." I could see the rage building behind her eyes again. "I had Ollie do it because I like to work on my images in the afternoon. I'm so stupid."

"Ollie – the kid with the gauges in his ears?" Lucas asked, trying to sound neutral. But from the look on his face, I could tell he was thinking what we were thinking, *Why would you trust that knucklehead with anything, much less bank deposits?* I'd talked with him several times, and while he was nice enough, he always seemed a little distracted.

Cate sighed. "Yep, he's the one. We never have much cash to deposit. A couple hundred dollars a day since our artists get paid directly. Mostly, it's just sales from the few gift items and rent from the artisans. I checked the account the first few times he went, and everything was good. Then, I kind of assumed we were fine. Apparently, we were not."

Walter adjusted his hips on the couch next to me. "So he just didn't turn in the transfer request for the mortgage payments and then withdrew the money that should have gone to the mortgage." He ran his fingers through his hair. "For a kind of dumb kid, that's a pretty smart move. You wouldn't even notice because the amount would have been the same in the account, unless you checked your mortgage statement, I mean."

I banged my wine glass onto the table. "But wouldn't the bank have warned you that you missed a payment? Or several? I mean they don't want to foreclose, right? It's not good money for them. So much better to get your mortgage payment and all that interest." I looked to Stephen for affirmation.

"Right. Foreclosure isn't profitable for the bank. It just staunches the hemorrhage of money from someone who doesn't pay. They definitely would have sent notices."

Daniel's voice was very tiny when he spoke. "I expect that Wilma had those sent by hand with Ollie."

"What?!" Cate was on her feet again, and I was glad when Lucas took her wine glass away. She had looked ready to throw it.

"That's what she did when I missed a payment for the shop." He looked at me quickly. "I had the flu and didn't get my transfer done in time. When I went in the next week to set things right, the teller handed me a late payment notice. No email. No call. Just a piece of paper."

"Probably too cheap to pay for the stamp, the old bat. So she probably gave the man who was stealing from you the notifications that would have let you know he was stealing. Unbelievable," Mart shouted.

Now I felt like throwing my wine glass.

"I think that's probably illegal," Walter said quietly. "A breach of confidentiality at least. That may be your best way forward here, Cate. A lawyer arguing that the bank failed in its due diligence." Walter had sold a very successful construction business in San Francisco when he and Stephen had recently moved to St. Marin's, so I expected he knew what he was talking about.

Mom and Dad had sat quietly through this whole exchange, but now Dad's voice was clear. "I've just texted Sheriff Mason. He's on his way over."

It took me a minute to figure out why Dad had asked the sheriff to come when this was clearly a business issue. Then I realized what he was saying. "Ollie is a thief," I whispered.

"Maybe. Maybe not," Dad said. "But it's time to hand this query over the authorities, don't you think?"

Daniel, Mart, Stephen, and Walter looked at me pointedly. I had a habit of doing a bit of investigating on my own, and my friends did not like it.

"Good idea, Dad." I stood and walked over to Cate. "We'll figure this out, Cate. The co-op is going to be fine."

She leaned her head on my shoulder, and I hoped I was right.

2

Sheriff Mason had been all business when he'd arrived a few moments later. He took Cate's statement and then mine about what I'd discussed with Henri. Then, he asked all of us if we might know where Ollie was.

Oddly enough, no one did. St. Marin's is a very small town, so while we may not know the minutiae of each other's days, we did usually know where each of us was likely to be at a given time. Pickle, Henri's husband's best friend, for instance, would likely be at the wings place down in Salisbury nursing one beer while he watched a baseball game. Max Davies, the owner of the French restaurant in town, was at his restaurant every Friday since that was often the biggest sales day of the week and he didn't trust his staff to manage without him. Elle, our friend who owned the local farm stand, often bragged about how Friday night was her date night with DCI Barnaby from *Midsomer Murders*. Any deviation – like the fact that Henri and Bear were at that fundraiser instead of the wings place – was also usually common knowledge.

So when no one could suggest where Ollie might be, a heavy

silence sank on the room. We looked at one another, hoping someone could offer something, but no one had any ideas. The longer the silence stretched, the more I realized how very little I had known about Ollie at all. In fact, I hadn't even known his name until that very night.

This void of information felt disconcerting, but it also made me feel guilty. Had I really not asked this guy his name on any of my visits to the co-op? I was really good at talking with people, so good that many folks thought I was an extrovert even though I was pretty high on the introvert scale. I did, however, have a deep interest in people and stories, so the fact that I had never bothered getting to know any of Ollie's stories, that bothered me.

"Okay," the sheriff sat back against the couch. "Tell me what you know about this guy."

Cate began pacing the living room. "His name is Oliver Blessing, at least that's what he told me—"

"Wait," the sheriff stopped taking notes. "Why do you say it like that?"

Cate stood in front of him. "Because if he stole from me, I don't trust anything he said."

The sheriff nodded. "Okay, fair enough. What else?"

I took a deep breath and waited.

"Nothing. I mean I have his social security number and stuff in our files since we had to get that to pay him. His address is there probably, too. But beyond that I don't know anything." She began pacing again and then stood in front of me. "That's weird, right, Harvey? I mean that I don't know anything about him."

I nodded. "I was just thinking the same thing. It's weird."

Daniel scooted closer beside me and picked up Aslan. This

whole thing was feeling hinky, and we needed a little cuddling for comfort.

The sheriff said, "Alright then. But maybe you know more than you think you do. Did you ever see what kind of car he drove?" He addressed his question to Cate but then looked around the room.

"I didn't," Cate said, "but now that you mention it, I don't think I ever saw him in a car. He biked everywhere."

Daniel nodded. "Yeah, I didn't see him with any kind of car." Daniel noticed every car, so this was certain confirmation of the no-car theory.

"So he biked to work. He must have lived in town," the sheriff said as he made a note.

Cate paused her pacing again. "No, I don't think so. He often came to work a little sweaty – not gross or anything – but like he'd been exerting himself. Now, I wonder if that meant he was biking some distance."

The sheriff continued to take notes. "About how old is he?"

Cate glanced at me. "You're better with ages than I am."

"If I had to guess, I'd say about twenty, twenty-five tops. The ear gauges made him seem young, but he wasn't a teenager. He kind of carried himself like he'd been out in the world a bit more, so to speak."

The sheriff winked at me. "Is that what we're calling "old" these days – out in the world?"

"Yes, yes we are," I said, lifting my chin snootily into the air.

"We're kind of missing the obvious, right?" Stephen asked with a small wave. "What did the guy look like?"

The sheriff nodded. "Thank you, Stephen. I wondered when we were going to get there."

"Oh, yeah, right. Tall, very thin. Curly, unkempt brown hair. And those ear gauges, not huge ones but big enough to stand out," Cate said.

The sheriff had his pen hovering over his paper like he was waiting for something.

"That's it. I mean I didn't notice any tattoos or anything." Cate looked puzzled.

"His race?" The sheriff's voice had just a bit of an edge to it. "Most of us," he looked at all of us in the room, "are prone to forget to describe someone's ethnicity if they are white. We act like being white is "normal." He shook his head just slightly.

Sheriff Mason Tucker was one of the very few black sheriffs in the state of Maryland, and I knew he'd caught more than his fair share of ugliness because of his ethnicity. He played off the hatefulness most of the time with wisecracks and a tendency to pull the best pranks on the Eastern Shore, but I imagined the specter of racism was never far away from him.

I sighed. "You're right, Tuck. Ollie is white. Sorry I didn't think to tell you."

The sheriff gave me a kind smile. "Thanks, Harvey." He stood. "I'll get in touch with Wilma Painter first thing in the morning and figure out the status of things at the bank. No need to go accusing anyone if this is just a paperwork error."

Daniel glanced up at the sheriff. "Have you ever known Wilma to make a paperwork error?"

Tuck let out a long sigh. "I have not. But still, better to get all my ducks in a row . . ." He headed for the front door.

My mom skittered into the kitchen and then back out. "A little thanks for coming out on a Friday night." She held two of Lucas's cupcakes on a paper plate.

"Just doing my job," the sheriff said, "but always happy to accept gratitude." He turned to Lucas. "Is this one of those strawberry-filled ones that Lu keeps telling me about?" Luisa, the sheriff's wife, ran the best taco truck on the Eastern Shore, and on Fridays, she'd started selling Lucas's cupcakes.

"It is. Hope you like it."

"Don't have to hope. Lu always saves me one, so this one will need to be our secret, okay?"

Lucas winked with a smile.

As soon as Sheriff Mason left, the group migrated to the kitchen to clean up and gather their things. We all knew there was nothing to do but wait.

WE DIDN'T HAVE to wait long, though. I had a a leisurely breakfast on the water with Stephen and Walter at the house they were renting until their contract closed in two weeks and by the time I got to the co-op about ten-thirty the next morning, , the sheriff had already been by to tell Cate what he knew.

Apparently, it had been four months since any payment had been applied against the mortgage for the co-op building, so the bank was well within its rights to begin foreclosure procedures. In some odd way, Wilma's warning to Henri had been a gift since it gave the co-op a heads up before the legal proceedings began.

"Still, she could have been more, I don't know, *friendly* about it," I said when Cate relayed that piece of info.

She nodded. "What I have to do is figure out how to bring our account back up to black. Fortunately, the co-op has some cash reserves, so we can do that. But it basically zaps our emergency fund. We'll just have to hope the building doesn't need any major repairs."

I groaned. "I'm glad you have the cash, but I know it's stressful to not have any backup. Hopefully, the sheriff can arrest Ollie soon. Maybe he hasn't spent the money yet?"

Cate rolled her eyes. "If you had stolen almost sixteen thousand dollars, would you have put it away for a rainy day?"

"Right. You may have a point." I had to admit that Ollie didn't strike me as the altruistic type. But then, he also didn't strike me as a hardened criminal either . . . or even a criminal with the forethought to plan such a heist. "Is the sheriff looking to at least arrest him?"

"I think the phrase he used was 'bring him in for questioning.'" Cate leaned against the counter at the front of the co-op. "I'm glad of that, but on top of all the missing money, that means I'm going to be down an employee—"

Just then, Ollie Blessing walked through the front door, tossed his messenger bag over the counter, and said, "Hi Boss," before proceeding to walk around and join Cate against the counter.

"Ollie, what are you doing here?"

He furrowed his brow. "I thought I was on the schedule for today."

Now it was Cate's turn to look puzzled. "Well, you were, but I didn't think you'd be back to work—"

I interrupted. "Ollie, did you hear about the kerfuffle over at the bank yesterday afternoon?"

He looked up toward the ceiling. "Oh yeah, Ms. Johnson said

that the lady with the leaky hair up at the bank had yelled at her. That woman can be really mean."

Cate and I stared at one another. "Ollie, someone has been stealing from the co-op. The mortgage hasn't been paid in months."

I wouldn't say that *shock* described the expression that crossed Ollie's face. *Mild surprise* maybe. *Befuddlement* perhaps. But no guilt. No defensiveness.

"That sucks, Boss. You okay?"

Cate looked at me again, and she was definitely shocked. "Ollie, the sheriff is looking for you."

"He is?" The more Ollie talked, the more he reminded me of the Keanu Reeves character from *Bill and Ted's Excellent Adventure.* Sweet but clueless. "Why?"

Cate's voice was just the slightest bit shrill. "Because you are the one who takes the mortgage payments to the bank every month, Ollie."

"I do?" Some level of worry seemed to be registering on Ollie's face at this point. "When?"

Cate let out an exasperated sigh. "When you take the deposit to the bank? The mortgage payment slip is in the envelope."

"It is?"

I couldn't take any more of this. Clearly, the guy had no idea what was going on. "Cate, I think we need to call the sheriff."

She gave a vigorous nod. "Ollie, don't go anywhere, okay?"

He nodded. "Sure thing, Boss. I'll be here, same as always."

Cate and I started to talk as we walked back to her studio around the corner. "A thieving mastermind might have been able to play the dumb kid part that well," I said, "but somehow, I don't think Ollie is a mastermind of that caliber."

For the first time since last night, Cate cracked a smile. "You can say that again." She stopped just before we stepped into her office and walked back a few steps to where she could see the front desk. "Ollie, do you drive?"

"Nope, Boss. Epilepsy. Not allowed."

"Oh, wow. Okay. Where do you bike in from?"

"Wye Mills," he said as if it was just the other end of the street. Wye Mills was over twenty miles away.

"You bike forty miles a day just to work here?"

He shrugged. "I like art."

Well, that was that. He liked art. I couldn't argue with that logic.

Cate caught up with the sheriff and told him what we'd learned. He said he'd be over to talk to Ollie, just to be sure, but that it sounded like we had to go at another angle. Cate looked deflated. Still, she walked me to the front door and then took up next to Ollie again.

As I walked out the front door, I heard her say, "Epilepsy. Do you have seizures often?" I smiled. Guess Cate was going to make right on the fact that none of us had taken the time to get to know this kid in our town. I'd have to do the same next time I was in.

THE DAY at the shop flew by. We were busier than ever now that the tourist season had started, and customers were at the register most of the day buying everything from local history books to these cute pocket journals that Rocky had suggested we carry. When closing time rolled around, I collapsed into the chair and a half by the history section and took a deep breath. Daniel and Lucas had headed over to Baltimore to see an Orioles game, and I had decided a night on my own sounded perfect. Mart was away consulting with a winery outside Harrisburg, Pennsylvania, and I didn't tell anyone else that Daniel was away. I was looking forward to a quiet walk home, a warm bath, and binge-watching *Glow Up* until I fell asleep.

I finished up the closing routine just as Rocky came over. "Hot date tonight, woman?" I asked, feigning innocence.

She blushed deeply and grinned. "Yep. Going to see a movie after we get dinner."

"Good," I said. "I'm happy for you two."

Rocky's smile almost reached her ears as she saw Marcus outside the door at her car. "See you tomorrow, Harvey."

I waved back, set the alarm, and put on Mayhem's leash. It was the perfect evening for a walk, and my girl knew it. She didn't even pull as we headed up Main Street past Max's restaurant. The sidewalk tables were full, and I was eager to move Mayhem along before she helped herself to someone's roll. But Max grabbed my arm, interrupting himself in the middle of taking a young couple's order.

"Harvey. It's wonderful to see you. You look absolutely lovely tonight." Max had a lingering crush on me, and despite my best efforts to convince him I was both committed to Daniel and completely uninterested in him, he persevered. On some microscopic level, I gave him credit for persistence.

"Thank you, Max. Have a good night." I picked up the pace and headed toward the other end of town.

We strolled past Daniel's shop and then out to the south edge of town before turning back through the residential streets near the library. Mayhem loved watching the kids on the playground,

and I was a big fan of the restored covered bridge at the end of
the park itself. It made me feel connected to history, tied to this
place in a way that even the old buildings on Main Street didn't.

As we crossed over the bridge, something caught my eye as it
fluttered in the wind. I thought it might be a piece of trash and
started to make my way down to grab it. I hated litter, and when
I could, I filled my pockets with discarded bottles and stray
newspaper pages. But as I got closer to the silvery object, I realized it wasn't a piece of paper. It was a scarf, and as my eyes
followed the scarf back up the bank by the bridge, they came to a
face.

I lost my footing and dropped to my butt on the bank. I had the
forethought not to scream since I didn't want to alarm the children on the swings just above us, but I did let out a shocked sob.
It was Wilma Painter from the bank, and she was dead.

Mayhem strained at her leash, eager to get to Wilma, but I
wrapped the leash around my ankle and pulled my phone from
my pocket. I dialed the sheriff's office directly – 911 sometimes
took longer. Harriet, the dispatcher, answered. I told her where I
was and what I'd found. "The sheriff needs to come now,
Harriet."

"Absolutely. I'm calling him now and sending the officer on duty
to you this moment." I could hear her say, "Covered bridge.
Murder," to someone in the room.

Even as she spoke, I heard the sound of the siren and suddenly
realized that my self-control about screaming was going to be
useless if a bunch of children got curious about the police arriv-
ing. I let Mayhem tug me up the hill to the swings and quickly
told the adults nearby that the police were on their way and that
it might be best for the children to not be here. I knew a lot of
these parents, grandparents, and nannies from the store, and
something in my face must have telegraphed the seriousness of

the situation because they nodded, didn't ask questions, and began moving the children away. From what I'd seen on the hillside near the body, I didn't think they could have seen anything from that angle, and we didn't need tiny eyes trying to get a look at what brought out the police car.

By the time the deputy arrived, the playground was empty, and I took a deep breath of relief. At least the trauma of this day wouldn't be inflicted on the youngest in our town. I led the deputy back down to Wilma's body and then took a step back.

Deputy Dillard was new to the police force in St. Marin's, and while I had met him a few times when he had come into the bookstore, I hadn't yet seen him in action. Unfortunately, something about his gangly frame and slightly pasty complexion always reminded me of Barney Fife, but he quickly dispelled my preconceived ideas that he might be a bumbling if loveable fool.

He immediately took Wilma's pulse and then gave me a little shake of his head. She was definitely dead. Then, he stood up and asked me to move back to the top of the hill so that we didn't disturb the scene any more than necessary. While I sat on the end of the covered bridge with Mayhem at attention next to my feet, the deputy strung police tape around the hillside in such a way that it would be seen clearly if you approached but barely noticeable from a distance. He definitely knew what he was doing.

Then, he went to his car and brought me back a bottle of water and a granola bar. "You've had a shock," he said kindly.

I felt tears spring to my eyes as I realized he was right. I let out a shuddery sob and took a sip of the water while he gazed across the playground, near but not intrusive as I gathered myself.

A few moments and the granola bar later, he turned back to me. "Are you able to tell me about this afternoon?"

I was a word person, so I immediately noticed that he didn't ask me to tell him what happened or about what I found. Only about my afternoon, because, of course, this was part of my afternoon.

I nodded, and he sat beside me on the edge of the bridge, notebook in hand. I told him about my walk through town and back out through the park. About coming down to get what I thought was a wrapper or piece of paper. About discovering it was Wilma's silver scarf and then finding her body.

"Okay. Then what?"

I sat up straighter. "Then nothing. I called Harriet, and here we are."

He smiled. "Right. But what did you do while you waited? You were at the top of the bank when I got here, so you must have climbed up, right? " He looked me in the eye. "Just thinking about the crime scene and footprints. Want to rule yours out."

I sighed. "Got it. Yes, I climbed back up and told the adults on the playground that a police car was on the way." When I saw his eyes narrow, I quickly said, "I didn't tell them why. But I did want them to be able to get the children away."

A slow smile spread across his face. "Good idea. Thanks for that, and thanks for not telling anyone about Ms. Painter. Word will spread fast enough without us helping it along."

Now, it was my turn to smile. He hadn't been here long, but he sure knew our town already. "You got that right? Familiar with small towns, are you?"

"Grew up in Princess Anne." He named an adorable town full of Victorian houses further down the Shore. "You couldn't get a haircut without it getting printed in the church bulletin."

"Here, it might not make the bulletin, but it will be the talk of the coffee hour after the service."

"Good to know," he said as he stood. "There's Sheriff Mason now."

I looked up to see the sheriff's pick-up coming into the parking lot on the other side of the park. Recently, Daniel had bought an old Chevy pick-up that he was restoring for me, and so I was particularly keen on old trucks. I still had a lot to learn, but I could tell this one was a Ford, probably sixties. A side-step in a rusty red. It shone in the afternoon sun, and when the sheriff stepped out in blue jeans and a ball cap, he looked right at home.

His face was serious when he walked up. "You found her, Harvey?" he asked quietly.

I nodded.

He looked down the bank then turned to Deputy Dillard. "Coroner will be here soon. Crime scene techs, too." He looked over at the swings. "Good work clearing the playground."

"Oh, that was all Harvey," the deputy tilted his head in my direction.

Tuck smiled. "Thanks for that. Dillard here got your statement?"

"He did." I stood and gathered most of Mayhem's leash in my hands. "I'll be at home tonight if you need me."

The sheriff gave my arm a squeeze and then turned back to his officer. They had work to do, and as much as I liked the sheriff, I wasn't thrilled to have to see him twice in less than twenty-four hours. Plus, I wanted to think through all this. I mean, it seemed far too coincidental that the day after Wilma threatens to fore-close on the co-op, she is killed.

Mayhem and I finished our walk across the bridge and up the backside of Main Street before cutting across toward home. I kept thinking about Ollie, about how he had seemed so clueless about what was going on, and I thought about doubling back and asking the sheriff what he'd learned when he questioned him that morning. But I knew the sheriff had more important things to do *and* that he would not take kindly to me inquiring about his investigation. Nope, I'd have to find out from Cate.

I picked up the pace on the last few blocks toward home, eager to call Cate and tell her about Wilma while also getting the low-down on Ollie, but when I reached our driveway, I saw my parents' car there. I wasn't expecting them, but now that they lived in town, maybe they'd just decided to stop by. I'd been intending to have a conversation about boundaries – like calling first before coming over – but my relationship with my mom and dad was the best it had been since I was a child and felt nervous about hurting their feelings when our connection felt really tender. Still, I was a little annoyed to find them there unannounced.

Mom was around the side of the house, weeding our planter boxes, and I considered slipping inside quietly, my tendency to want to avoid my parents still strong. But Mayhem had other ideas and let out an excited bark as we approached. Mom looked up and smiled, which made me feel guilty. She was happy to see me, and I needed to be happy to see her, too.

I smiled back. "Thanks for weeding. That was on my schedule for this afternoon, but I got waylaid."

Mom looked at me closely. "Are you okay?"

For not the first time in my life, I wished that I actually had a poker face, or even a rummy face, but I was never good at hiding how I was feeling. "Yeah, I am. Just made a hard discovery on the way home." I sighed. "Come have a glass of wine. I'll tell you about it."

She nodded. "Alright. I can't stay long, though. Your dad is grilling out, and you know how he gets if his monthly night of cooking isn't treated with the utmost honor." She gave me a small smile, but then jutted out her chin. "If you need us, though, Harvey, I can call him and let him know to put the steaks on hold."

"No, no. I don't want you to miss Dad's steaks, but I think you'll want to hear this."

We made our way into the bungalow, and I poured us each a glass of pinot grigio, which we carried to the small patio behind the house. I took a sip and said, "You remember that woman we were talking about last night, the banker?"

"Wilma something?"

"Right, Wilma Painter. Mayhem and I just found her body over by the covered bridge."

Mom set her glass down hard on the patio table. "You what?"

"Right. The sheriff is there now." I put my head down on the table by my wine glass.

I felt Mom's cool hand on the back of my neck and then heard her lift her glass again. "That must have been a shock."

"It was." I sighed. "But I can't help but think that there's some connection to what's happening at the co-op."

Mom sat up very straight. "That's why I came by. I almost forgot. I ran into Cate when I was at Elle's farm stand. The sheriff has cleared Ollie, which is good news. Right?"

I let out of a long, slow breath. "Definitely. But that means we have no idea who was stealing from the co-op, which isn't good news? And now, we need to figure out who killed Wilma."

Most of my friends would have stopped me right there and noted that *we* needed to do no such thing, but Mom didn't say a word. I had clearly gotten my curiosity from her, even if she had lectured me not to be nosy almost every day of my childhood.

"True. But Cate also said that the sheriff had some other lines of inquiry to pursue." Mom averted her eyes.

"There's something you're not telling me." I leaned forward and placed my hand on hers. "Mom, what is it?"

"Well, I guess they're looking into Henri Johnson. Seems there's some question about whether she might be involved."

I let my body fall back against the chair. "What?! No. There's no way. Henri was stupefied about this yesterday. Plus, what would be her motivation? She's married to a doctor, for Pete's sake. And the co-op benefits her, I mean that's where she works and sells—"

Mom held up a hand. "I know, Harvey. You don't have to convince me. I'm just sharing what I heard at the salon." My mother got her hair cut and dyed once a month like clockwork. I had forgotten this was the Saturday.

I sighed and tried to let my shoulders drop back down and away from my ears. "You're right. Of course." I leaned back and stared at the perfect blue sky. "This just sucks."

I heard Mom take another sip of wine. "It does. Royally."

MOM HEADED HOME a few minutes later, and I called in an order of take-out from the Thai place in town. Tonight called for pad Thai and I decided I'd follow it up with a batch of peanut butter popcorn.

I plopped into my reading chair. When the food arrived thirty minutes later, I was in my cute but very comfy plaid PJ pants, an oversized T-shirt, and the bear slippers Daniel had bought me for our two-month dating anniversary.

I dropped onto the couch with takeout containers, banishing Aslan to the chenille throw at the other end of the sofa. Just as I started to queue up all the greatness that is a reality show makeup competition, Cate rang the bell. She was in sweats and a T-shirt that had more than the required number of holes, and she had a headband tucked up around her straight, black hair. "I didn't feel like being alone," she said.

I pointed toward the containers and the TV. "Come on in."

Cate gave me the firsthand update on events, and I listened attentively, not feeling it necessary or helpful to let her know Mom had already filled me in. "The sheriff is going to get an earful from Bear – probably Pickle – too. He must have some serious information if he's even considering going that route."

Bear, Henri's husband, was an ER surgeon here in town, and his best friend, Pickle, was an attorney. The two came off as a pair of good ole boys what with their affection for gas-station chicken and storytelling, but they were both well-educated, well-respected men, men who didn't tolerate fools.

"Well, this is mostly hearsay, I guess. I mean, the sheriff might have just been telling me stuff to make me feel better."

I dropped my head to my chin and gave her a pointed look. "When have you ever known Sheriff Mason to let out any information that wasn't true. You know how careful he is with releasing information. He must have a good reason."

I curled my knees up to my chin and chewed my lip. "I'm missing something. I just know it."

Cate rolled her eyes. "You do love to build up a mystery, don't you, Harvey Beckett?"

"That's why you love me." I stretched my legs back out and slipped my feet under my friend's legs.

"Among the many reasons." She smiled, and I found myself very glad that she'd come over. "Now, I know you had planned on a makeup show binge, but I'm thinking *Veronica Mars* might be a better choice," she looked at me out of the corner of her eyes.

I sat forward and looked back at her. "Are you serious? Sleuthing and teenage love triangles? I can't imagine anything better."

3

*S*unday morning was probably my favorite time of the week. Everyone moved a little more slowly with fewer plans and more space in their day. The store was quiet, too, since most of the folks in St. Marin's spent the first part of the day at church. I liked the silence, the visits from a few regulars coming for coffee or just to browse, the tourists who wandered in with their bellies full from any one of the wonderful B&Bs around town, and time to just think about the week ahead.

This week, though, I was preoccupied. I was trying to guess at Tuck's plan when the man himself came in. He and Lu were regular attendees at the Episcopal Church outside of town, and he was clearly on his way there – his khaki pants, salmon shirt, and bright blue tie a nice departure from his uniform or blue jeans and polo attire. Lu looked lovely in a draping, flowered dress with a bright yellow headband that complemented her dark brown hair and olive skin.

"You guys are gorgeous. Like an advertisement for spring. What brings you by?"

Lu gave me a wink. "Well, I'm here for a cinnamon roll, but I think Tuck wanted to talk about something with you." She gave her husband's shoulder a squeeze. "I'll be back in a minute." She headed toward the café, where Rocky was waiting with a fresh plate of her mom's amazing cinnamon rolls. I made a mental note to snag one before they were all gone.

The sheriff gave me a mischievous grin as he glanced around the shop. "Got a minute to talk in the back."

"Ooh, a mystery. I like that." The shop was pretty empty, and I caught Rocky's eye. She gave me a thumbs up. "Let's go."

We stepped into the storage room at the back of the shop, and Tuck and I took seats on stacks of boxes. "What's up?" I asked.

"I need your help." Tuck's voice was quiet and serious.

I leaned forward toward my friend and said, "I'm sorry. Could you repeat that?" In the past, the sheriff had been none too keen on my curious investigations, so this was a surprising and wonderful turn of events.

"Don't get too excited. You don't need to be doing any police work. I just need your help to, well, lay a trail."

I jumped up and pumped the air with my fist. "I knew it. You don't really suspect Henri. It's a trap."

He stood up and put his hands in front of him. "Not a trap, Harvey – entrapment is illegal – a trail. You need to understand that. We aren't trying to trick anyone, just lead them out, okay?" His voice was very stern.

I took a deep breath. "Right. A trail. Okay, how do I help?"

"I take it the rumor already reached you that I am looking at Henri Johnson as a person of interest. That's the first step. Now, I need you to help me convince everyone that she is guilty."

My enthusiasm for my part in this trail-blazing waned considerably. "Tuck—"

"Don't worry. Henri and Bear – even Pickle – are in the know. But besides Lu, me, and now you, no one else can know. Not even Daniel. For this to work, people have to believe I'm looking for evidence to arrest Henri. Okay?"

I was liking this plan less and less, especially if it meant keeping secrets. But I reminded myself that a murderer was on the loose. "Okay, what do I need to do?"

"Simple. You have to convince everyone that I'm convinced about Henri's guilt. You can even *pretend* to be looking for evidence against her. Everyone you know will believe that you're caught up in the investigation. It's true to your nature."

I paused and then I felt my mood lift. "You want me to investigate the crime publicly while you do the same privately? I can do that." I gave him a grin.

The sheriff shook his head, but I saw a smile lift the corner of his mouth. "Pretend to investigate, Harvey. Just throw the killer off with your sleuthing, okay? Keep the attention on you and away from me."

"Permission to sleuth. I'm totally in."

He sighed. "But because you're going to be the focus, we need to be sure you're safe, so Deputy Dillard is going to be working with you. That way, you'll have protection."

I nodded. I liked our new deputy, and I thought this might be a lot of fun . . . and a satisfying way to feed my curiosity. "Got it. But this is pretty elaborate, Tuck. Why all the cloak and dagger?"

He looked off into the middle distance. "I'm not sure yet. Something tells me, though, that this killer is very careful, and I want to employ every resource – you included," he gave my shoulder a little nudge, "to catch them."

"It probably helps that I found Wilma's body, huh?" Remembering her blue face sobered my enthusiasm a bit. I hadn't liked the woman, but murder was horrible no matter who it happened to.

"It does. It allows us the ruse that you already know some basics like cause and time of death since you were there at the crime scene."

"Right. Except, of course, I don't know those things." I wiggled my eyebrows, trying to play the farcical sleuth but feeling a little ·queasy remembering Wilma's body draped across that bank.

He proceeded to tell me that Wilma had been strangled with her own scarf, that the killer must have snuck up on her and dragged her down the hill.

"Must have been someone strong then?" I asked.

"Maybe. But Wilma wasn't very strong, and she was in heels. Once she was off the paved path, it probably wouldn't have been too hard for even a weaker person to get her off her feet, especially if they had grabbed her by the neck."

I tried not to picture it. "Okay, and when?

"Coroner says about ten yesterday."

I shuddered. Wilma had been murdered in broad daylight near where children were playing. This killer was ballsy and cold.

"You can see why discretion is required and why I need your help. We're not talking about a heat of the moment thing, Harvey. Wilma took that walk every Saturday morning on the way to visit her mother at the nursing home on the north side of town. The killer knew that. They waited for her."

I wrapped my arms tight and hugged myself. "Wilma's mother lives in town? I didn't know that. I haven't seen her around, I don't think."

"You probably wouldn't. From what I gather, she's bedridden and has a pretty advanced case of dementia." He rubbed his forehead. "Pretty kind of Wilma to visit every week even so, though."

I sighed. "I'd say. Do you have suspects?" At this point I couldn't tell if I was asking for my own "investigation" or because I really hoped the sheriff would nab this person quickly.

"I do, but I'm not going to tell you anything about that – both because it would be unwise for the sake of our investigation but also because it'll make it more believable for your performance."

I nodded. "Can I ask one more question?"

He gave me one crisp nod.

"Ollie isn't a suspect, right?"

He looked at me somberly. "I'm not ruling anyone out, Harvey. Not anyone."

After the sheriff and Lu left for church, I found Mayhem and took the chair next to her in the psychology section. If I couldn't talk to my friends, at least I had her. I gave her ear a scratch, and she looked up at me quizzically. "No one is going to like this, are they girl?"

She licked my hand.

"Thanks. I knew you'd understand. Now, where do we start?"

I SPENT the day pondering my sleuthing tactics when I wasn't recommending books or ringing up customers. I knew I had to be subtle, so I couldn't go all Poirot and question everyone who might have motive. Besides, I didn't even know who had motive. No, this had to look like my usual routine of following hunches.

Midafternoon, two young women came in and headed right for the self-help section. One of them looked familiar, but in a town as small as St. Marin's, everyone is familiar after you've been here a couple of weeks.

But when they came to the counter with their purchases – *Crazy Rich Asians* and *Why Didn't They Teach Me This in School?* – I realized that one of the women was Cynthia, the teller at the bank. Her hair was down, and she was in a hoodie instead of her bankish blouse and trousers, but it was definitely her. I smiled and said, "Hey Cynthia. It's good to see you."

She smiled. "Hi, Ms. Beckett. Good to see you, too." She held up the books. "Good?"

I didn't know the Siegel book that well – being a reader a bit older than his target demographic – but I'd heard good things. And I loved Kwan's books. "Yep. Great choices." I looked past her to the woman standing behind her. "Hi, I'm Harvey."

Cynthia looked back. "Oh yeah, sorry. This is Ariel. We work together. She mostly works in loans, so maybe you guys haven't met."

Ariel stepped up, gave a guarded smile, and put out her hand. "Nice to meet you. I like your store."

"Thanks, Ariel. You guys headed somewhere fun after this?"

Cynthia nodded. "It's so beautiful outside. We thought we'd head over to the marina and get some oysters."

I cringed. "Ooh, well, you can have my portion. Can't stand the things."

Ariel eyed me carefully. "Not from around here then?"

"Actually, I am. Just up in Chesapeake City. Seafood and I just don't like each other much." I always felt awkward saying that here in this town that the seafood industry still supported in part and where crabs were not only a beloved meal but also the state animal.

The girls shrugged. "More for us then," Cynthia said warmly.

I finished ringing up their sale and then said, quietly, "I heard about what happened to Wilma. I'm so sorry."

Cynthia looked down at her hands. "Yeah, she wasn't always easy to work with, but . . ."

"Yeah, you never wish that on anyone," I finished.

"Wait, weren't you the one who found her body?" Ariel's voice had an edge to it, and I looked over at her quickly.

"I was."

The young woman was scowling. "So why'd you say you heard about it? You did more than hear, it seems like."

Cynthia put a hand on her friend's arm. "It's just a figure of speech."

"Exactly. Plus, you can understand why I wouldn't really want everyone to know I was the one who found her. I mean, in case they thought I knew more than I did or something." I was treading a thin line here, trying to imply that I did know more while looking like I didn't. Subterfuge was complicated.

Ariel studied my face. "Oh, okay. Well, yeah, I guess I can see that."

"Anyway, the sheriff has a suspect, so, hopefully, this will be all wrapped up soon." I figured now was as good a time as any to start laying that trail.

Both women looked at me then. "Oh?" Cynthia said, "I thought you and Henri were friends."

I bit my lip, willing my brain to get going.

"We are, but a crime is a crime, right?" Just the sound of those words coming out of my mouth made me a little queasy. I was the last person someone would call a "law and order" type.

"Oh, well, then . . ." Cynthia's voice was thin and nervous. I probably sounded a little aggressive.

I swallowed and tried not to think about Tuck. He would not be happy that I had started before Deputy Dillard was on board, but I couldn't pass up this opportunity. "Justice will prevail."

I tried to smile warmly. "Enjoy the oysters, girls."

They walked out, and the bell over the door rang softly as I watched them walk up the street. Now, there were two women with means and opportunity to steal, I thought. How hard would it be for a bank employee to just shred those transfer papers, I wondered?

Then, I chuckled to myself. "Justice will prevail," I said quietly. I sounded like a movie trailer.

WHEN CLOSING TIME CAME, I was exhausted more from the scheming than from the actual bookstore work, and I dreaded my Sunday night wine and garden time with Mart, Cate, and Elle. That is, until I decided this was my chance to try my hand at upping my acting skills. If I could fool them, I could fool anyone.

Unlike our Friday night potlucks, which rotated from house to house each week, the women and I always met at our house on Sundays. Mart brought the wine, of course, and we all enjoyed gardening. Technically, the garden belonged to Mart and me since it was in our yard but, in actuality, we considered it a group project.

Elle, of course, had the most knowledge, so she was our leader.

I'd grown up with a small garden – tomatoes, peppers, herbs – at my childhood home, and Cate's mother had grown a plethora of vegetables on their little patio in New York City. Mart, however, had no experience with plants, not even house plants. "My thumbs are so black I could apply football player's grease paint," she said.

As Mart filled our glasses in the cooling evening light, we each took to our little plots of soil. Cate had a beautiful patch of Korean radishes – a tribute to her heritage – that Lucas would use in their meals, and her scallions looked amazing. "I think your parents would be proud," I said as I headed over to weed my own carrots.

"Thanks, Harvey," she said. "Now remember, those frilly tops, those are the carrots you intentionally planted. Don't weed them out again."

I gave her my best exasperated stare, but then bent to the task. I had weeded out, accidentally, not one but two patches of carrots already this spring. As I took a glance at Mart's end of our bed, I saw that so far, her broccoli plants were looking healthy, and her cabbages looked downright market-worthy. My dear but uninformed best friend had wanted to go right in with tomato plants in mid-April, but thank goodness Elle tactfully noted that our last frost wasn't until early May. "Tomatoes like heat, my dear. Lots of heat. Let's wait until Mother's Day, just to be safe." Mart had nodded, thankful, I think, for an explanation. She was a keen learner . . . and a really observant person. I didn't know if I could fool her with my murder-distracting ploy, but it was time to give it a shot.

"You all heard about Henri, right?" I said, trying to sound casual.

Elle harvested the most perfect leaves of kale off the gorgeous, blue-green plants she'd been babying since they were seeded.

The woman had an entire farm to tend, but still, she came here every Sunday to help us out . . . and I suspected she appreciated the company, too. I imagined I'd be kind of lonely out there on thirty acres with just my animals for companionship. She loved what she did, though. You could see it in her face.

Now, though, her face grew stormy. "I did, and that's BS. I mean, I respect Tuck and all, but he's so off-base on this one it's not even funny."

BS was pretty strong language for Elle, who felt profanity was the resource of the small-minded. I was glad she hadn't yet been around when I dropped something on my foot.

Cate said, "I can't even believe it." She slid a soil-covered hand across her cheek. "The sheriff knows Henri, too. Surely, he knows better."

I took a deep breath and swallowed hard. "I mean, I don't know, but what if she did do it?"

Three faces whipped in my direction. "Harvey, you can't be serious. You know Henri. You know what kind of person she is." Elle's voice was full of hurt, like I'd just said I thought she was a murderer.

"I know. I do, but I saw how Wilma lit into her. It was ugly. I mean, I don't condone killing, but I could see how she might have been, well, tempted." I couldn't really see that at all – Henri was the most cool-headed, even-tempered person I knew. But I had to play my part, and this part relied on me selling my lie. "Goodness knows, there but for the grace of God . . ." I let my voice trail off as I carefully avoided pulling up a carrot.

Mart walked over to me. "Harvey, what is going on with you? You aren't being serious right now, are you?" Her face was full of concern.

I almost cracked right then, but I remembered that Tuck had said

Henri was in on the ruse. So I sighed and doubled-down. "Of course, I want Tuck to have evidence, but it does sound like she's the most likely suspect."

Cate flicked her hand trowel down into the dirt. "I can't take this. I'm going home. Mart, Elle, thank you for a lovely night. Harvey, well, I just don't know what to say." She walked slowly back to her car, her head down and shoulders hunched. I felt terrible.

Elle straightened up and stretched. "I think things here are in pretty good shape." She was trying to keep her voice light, I could tell, but I could also hear the quaver behind it. I recognized that tremble because it was the way my voice sounded anytime I was about to cry. "I'm going to be headed home, too."

I looked over at Mart. She was glaring at me. Then, she turned, gave Elle a wave, gathered the wine glasses, and went inside without a word.

I felt a lot like the manure we'd turned into these beds a few weeks ago. Apparently, I was a good liar. Too bad it had cost me my friends to find that out.

Mayhem was laying at the edge of the garden, waiting for me to be done so she could go inside and lay on *her* bed, the soft kind. "This sucks, girl." She wagged her tail in commiseration, but whether she was showing sympathy for the awful feeling in my belly or her dirty resting accommodations I couldn't be sure. "Let's go inside."

She didn't hesitate and was on her feet and heading toward the door before I could even get out of the planter box. I took my time going in, not eager to encounter Mart. But when I reached the door, she was there, two wine glasses and a fresh bottle in hand. "Harvey Beckett, you may have been able to fool those other women, but did you think you could fool me?"

I almost tripped on the door sill. "What?! What are you talking about?" I could hear how unconvincing I sounded.

"You are no more capable of believing an innocent person guilty than you are of convincing me of one of your lies. What in the world is going on?" She pointed to the couch and poured us each a glass of wine while she walked. I would never in a million years achieve that without at least spilling the wine. More likely, though, I'd trip, spill the wine, break the glasses, and cut open my hand. Grace had never been – and would never be – my forte.

I took a long sip from my glass. "What gave me away?"

"You want a list?"

I stared at her. "That bad?"

"That bad. Let's start with the 'I mean.' You only say that when you're trying to convince someone of something that you feel kind of bad trying to convince them of. Then, there's the fact that you wouldn't make eye contact with anyone. Plus, the tell where you try to push your glasses up on your face even though you have your contacts in—"

"Okay, okay," I interrupted. "I get it. You knew. But you can't tell anyone, no one, okay?"

"Tell them what, Harvey? I don't know what on earth is going on."

Aslan climbed into my lap, and for one moment I thought she was maybe offering comfort. But then she began pitty-pattying with her tiny pinprick claws that went *right* through my yoga pants, and I realized this was, of course, about her. Typical cat.

"Okay, but really, you can't say anything."

Mart dropped her chin and stared hard at me. "Got it. Now spill."

Over the bottle of wine, I told Mart about Tuck's plan, and when I was done, she clapped. "I didn't think we had much made-for-TV stuff here in our sleepy little town, but this is good enough for one of those police dramas with the actors who are far too attractive to be able to be inconspicuous. I love it, and I'm in."

I laughed but then swallowed. "Mart, I don't know. This cannot get out."

"I know. But I lie better. At least let me tell your parents and Daniel. You know they won't buy your lies for a second."

She had a point, and so I agreed to let Mart spread the rumor that I believed Henri was guilty of murder. "You have to sell it, Mart."

My friend stood and held the empty bottle of wine over her head. "We just doubled the price of this bottle of wine by putting a new, metallic label on it." I glanced up at the shiny stag's head on the label. "I can sell anything."

I sighed. She could, and she would.

SHE WASTED NO TIME EITHER. By lunchtime on Monday, Mom had texted to ask if I had a high fever that was causing me to be delusional, and Daniel had insisted on having tacos so we could talk about what I was thinking. He didn't look happy – in fact, he looked kind of peeved, and Daniel wasn't easily peeved. Once again, I felt terrible.

Then, I began to worry. Was this kind of deception dangerous to our relationship? I mean I was lying to him. I had hoped he would just avoid the subject, but at lunch, he said, "Do you really think Henri did this?" And I had to lie. Boldly. It felt awful.

Compound that with the fact that I was also still mulling over

the bank employees and considering doing a little digging –
quietly – into their relationships with Wilma, an act that Daniel
would wholeheartedly disapprove of, and I was fairly certain I
was sending an amazing thing right down the toilet.

By late afternoon, I felt so horrible about my deception that I
thought about going to the station and telling Tuck I couldn't go
through with it. I would have done it, too, I think, but then
Deputy Dillard stopped by.

He was out of uniform, but I wasn't sure if that was because he
was trying to look casual or because he was actually casual. He
had on Dad jeans – a little too acid-washed to be cool – and a
novelty T-shirt of Ramen noodles. "Nice shirt," I said.

"Thanks. My mom bought it for me. I love Ramen."

"Your mom knows you well." I chuckled.

He smiled. "You doing okay?" He started walking toward the
nature section, which struck me as funny given that those ramen
noodle packets that you can buy for forty-nine cents are about as
far from natural as you can get.

"Aside from the gut-eating guilt and sheer terror that I'm
leading my love life into the crapper, yep, I'm doing fine."

He winced. "Ugh. That's rough. Not a deception-prone person
then?"

I shook my head.

"An admirable quality, in my estimation." He pulled a fly-
fishing book by Jay Zimmerman off the shelf and started flipping
through the pages. "So other than heart-breaking guilt, no
trouble."

"Nope, nothing. Just normal business here."

"Good." He paused at a picture of what looked like a giant wooly worm to me. "I'm not sure why Tuck wanted me to ask this, but here goes. Are you considering doing any investigating yourself?"

I chuckled. The sheriff did know me well. "Not particularly."

The deputy looked up from his book. "That's not a no."

I blushed. "No, it's not."

He whistled. "Alright, so what you got?"

I pondered playing it off, trying to make more eye contact and avoid touching my face in any way, but then I decided it was better I just fess up. I couldn't do deception for two different purposes. "Yesterday, two bank employees came in." I told him about Cynthia and Ariel and how I had been wondering if they might have been able to pull off this kind of thing.

He tucked the book under his arm and pulled out his phone. "Probably worth looking into." Then he looked up at me. "By us, I mean. Not you." Then he studied my face. "That's why the sheriff wanted me to ask, isn't it? You have a tendency to do a little, um, investigating?"

I looked away, which was answer enough I guess.

"We'll look into it, Harvey. Meantime, keep spreading the word. We're getting somewhere, and as best we can tell, no one knows that."

I felt my heart pick up the pace a bit. "Getting somewhere? Meaning you have a suspect?"

Dillard took the book out from under his arm and headed toward the register. "Tuck said you liked questions."

"I guess that means you're not going to answer," I said as I rang up his purchase.

"Thanks for the book, Harvey. I'll be back tomorrow to check in, but you have my cell. Don't hesitate."

I felt slightly chastened when the deputy left, but I knew he was just doing his job. Still, I wondered who they were investigating.

DANIEL CAME by as I was locking up. "Walk you home?" he said quietly.

"I'd like that," I said, with the hopes that the tension from our lunch conversation would be gone. It wasn't, but at least he had come by.

We walked a few blocks with Taco twisting his leash around Mayhem, and Mayhem trying to make me need shoulder surgery. Neither of us spoke. I wasn't sure what to say that wouldn't make things worse.

Finally, he took Mayhem's leash and then held my hand. "Harvey, you and I may disagree about Henri's guilt, but I know you must have your reasons. I trust you."

I felt like someone had shoved a baseball down my throat. He trusted me when I was deliberately deceiving him. I couldn't take it.

I stopped walking and felt my arm pull as he took another step ahead before turning back. "I can't do this. I don't believe Henri is guilty."

"You don't? Then, why would you say that you did?" He looked sad, disappointed.

"Because the sheriff asked me to."

Daniel pursed his lips. "He did?"

"Yes, yesterday, and he made me promise not to tell even you or Mart."

A small smile peaked out the corner of his mouth. "Mart figured it out, didn't she?"

I jerked my head back. "How did you know?"

"It's all making sense now." He squeezed my hand and pulled me down the sidewalk. "She was really putting on a show in the shop earlier when she came in for the oil change she obviously didn't need. I thought she just wanted to vent, but now I see—"

"She was lying for me." I sighed. "I'm so sorry." I tried to stop him so I could show him how concerned I was, but he kept walking.

At first, I thought he was angry, but then I noticed a little bounce in his step. "You're not mad?"

"Nope."

I walked a bit further, trying to figure out what was going on. "I would be mad."

"Well, I'm not."

A few steps further and then I dragged all four of us to a stop again. "Okay, what's going on? You aren't mad at all?

He turned toward me then and took both of my hands in his. "I'm not mad, Harvey. Maybe a little hurt, but mostly I'm happy."

I raised one eyebrow. "Happy?"

"Yep. Because the way I see it, you couldn't bring yourself to lie to me. First you had Mart do it, and then, you couldn't even hold up her lies." He turned and started back down the road. "I like that. Means you care about what I think."

"Of course I care about what you think. More than I care about what anyone thinks. I didn't like this idea from the start, or at least I didn't like the lying part, but I knew the sheriff wouldn't ask if it wasn't important."

"Agreed. And I totally understand why you agreed. He needed your help, and you like to help."

I couldn't disagree.

"Plus, this way, there's the added win that you can't be all sleuth about other possible killers. You have to play this role."

I paused and then said, "Right."

This time, Daniel stopped. At this rate, we would never get to my house. "Harvey? You aren't looking into potential killers are you?"

I sighed. "I had some ideas, but I shared them with Deputy Dillard. No sleuthing for me. The undercover gig is too important."

It was Daniel's turn to sigh, and we resumed our walk. We were almost out of town when a bicycle whizzed by going north on Main Street toward Route 13. It was Ollie Blessing, and he was flying.

Before I even thought about it, I shouted, "Be careful, Ollie. Don't go so fast that the cars can't see you."

He looked back over his shoulder and waved. "You got it, Ms. B."

I waved to him slowly as he sped further away, but then I turned to Daniel. "The only other person who calls me Ms. B is Marcus." I studied his face for a moment. "It's not sleuthing if I just ask if they know each other, right?"

Daniel squinted one eye. "As long as it's actual curiosity, not investigation."

"Definitely." I meant that. Well, at least I wanted to.

4

*T*he next morning, Marcus and I both opened. New books were released on Tuesdays, and we both enjoyed the excitement of getting those new books on the shelf and selling the special orders to the die-hard fans. This week, N. K. Jemisin's new speculative fiction book was out, and we had several orders for it. The interest had been so high that we'd offered to host a discussion group at the end of the month for readers. So far, we already had twelve sign-ups.

Reworking our new book tables and shelves gave me the perfect opportunity to not-so-casually mention that Ollie had called me Ms. B the night before.

"Oh yeah, I was telling him about you. He's a big reader, too, but mostly from the library. Kind of tight on cash." Marcus was actually casual when he shared that information, but of course he would be because he knew nothing about the fact that Ollie was a suspect in Wilma's murder.

"Oh yeah. How do you know him?" I tried to convince myself I was just making conversation, but in my heart of hearts, I knew I was sleuthing. Daniel would be disappointed in me. Still, I couldn't seem to help myself.

"We went to college together. Dropped out together, too. It just didn't take for either of us."

I nodded. "He told me he liked art."

"He does. He's actually really talented. He does these mixed media pieces with found paper and fabric. Sort of graffiti-inspired but really amazing. I know he's hoping that working at the co-op will give him a chance to get some studio space there."

As I finished the last few displays at the front of the store, I thought about Ollie as an artist. He certainly looked the part, and I wondered if his cluelessness might be a bit of an act, a façade he wore to protect himself maybe. I'd done that for a lot of my life, pretended I didn't care much about something – my work, the books I loved, my friends – when really I cared so very much.

Or if he was acting, it could be a deliberate deception. The question was, how did I figure out what exactly was going on behind those bright red gauges in his ears?

"Marcus," I shouted as he headed back to the storeroom with our empty boxes. "Think Ollie might be willing to show me and a couple of friends some of his work?"

He shrugged. "Probably, especially if someone might buy something."

I grinned. "You know Stephen and Walter have all those big walls to fill."

Marcus laughed. "They do. I'll text Ollie in a minute, see if he can bring some stuff by sometime."

"Thanks!"

Either way, whether he was a starving and scared artist or a not-so-starving and scared thief, we'd get a chance to know our suspect just a bit more. I kept feeling like there was far more than meets the eye to Ollie Blessing.

THE QUICKNESS and eagerness of Ollie's reply to Marcus's text seemed to confirm my first sense – that he was innocent and feigning – or maybe just actually a bit oblivious. He was so excited that he offered to bring things in the next morning when he came in for his shift. Well, what he said was that he could bike home, pick up a couple of pieces, and bike back during his lunch break, but that felt extreme, especially for a potentially bogus sales opportunity. Plus, I needed time to prep Stephen and Walter for their roles.

My two friends were always nervous about my sleuthing, too, but they also had a spirit of adventure. I knew they'd get it . . . and they were also big art supporters, so if they could actually buy art and help a young artist, I knew they would.

Sure enough, when I filled them in over barbecue sandwiches at Piggle and Shake during dinner that night, they were on board. Of course, it helped that they still thought I suspected Henri of the murder. At least I had been able to fool somebody, but then, that was only because I'd let Mart tell them. Now, I was just hoping they wouldn't bring up the murder.

I told them Ollie was the young man from the co-op, that I felt bad that I hadn't gotten to know him more, and that Marcus said he was talented. That's all it took. Like me, my friends liked to help when they could, and their recent move from San Francisco to our slightly economically depressed Eastern Shore had left them in good stead financially. They weren't wild with their money, but they had it to spend if they wanted to spend it.

"Oh, I hope it's good," Stephen said. "I have a tendency to shop out of guilt."

Walter rubbed circles on his husband's back. "That's why you have me. I feel no guilt in saying no, even to a very nice, very in-need person."

"Good. I'm not looking for charity here. Just a chance to get to know Ollie a bit. Maybe I'll even think about giving him a show in the shop soon."

Stephen spewed his Dr. Pepper. "Where, Harvey?"

"In my shop," I repeated.

"No, I mean where would you hang the pieces. You have filled every square inch of that store's wall space with bookshelves. You couldn't display a collectible spoon in there."

He was right. Sometimes my desire to help overrode my logic circuits. "Well, maybe I can talk with Cate and see if he can get a studio in the co-op if I help sponsor it. Maybe then he could live here in town. Did I tell you that he bikes from Wye Mills every day?"

Walter smiled. "Harvey, you are too kind for your own good. I don't look at your account books, but I know you can't have that much to spend. Let us help Ollie, if we agree that his work warrants some support." He looked at Stephen. "We might get to be art patrons."

"The Medicis of our time," Stephen beamed.

"Didn't the Medicis kill people they didn't like and turn on each other, too?" I said.

"Don't be such a spoilsport what with your history and all that, Ms. Beckett." Stephen feigned a pout.

I laughed. "Thanks, guys. I really appreciate this. He'll be at the store at noon during his lunch break."

"We'll be there."

The guys looped up to our house and dropped me off before heading back to their waterfront house south of town. The moon was full, and I imagined the view from their back deck was amazing. It wasn't the first time I had been jealous of their house, but then, I was glad I got to visit there as much as I wanted.

WEDNESDAY MORNING'S opening was easy. Just one customer waiting for coffee, a tourist here for the week who had come to appreciate our locally roasted beans. She also picked up a cozy mystery each day – today's choice was *Poison in Paddington* by Samantha Silver – so I imagined she was relaxing and reading by the water somewhere. It sounded like a delightful way to spend a vacation.

No sooner had she left with her giant cappuccino and paperback than my parents stormed in. My mother was doing what I thought of as her catwalk stomp, the walk that Tyra Banks always taught the women on *America's Next Top Model*, all vim and vigor and just a taste of anger.

"Anastasia Lovejoy Beckett, what are you thinking? You cannot possibly believe that Henri Johnson murdered that woman."

Clearly my decision to ignore the increasingly intense barrage of texts questioning both my physical and mental health had made my mother a wee bit angry. She'd never liked my nickname Harvey, but she only pulled out the three full names when she was really peeved.

"It's nice to see you, too, Mom. What brings you in today?"

My father cleared his throat. "Your mother thought it important," he gave me an exaggerated shrug from where he stood behind her, "to make it clear that we find it horrible that you would betray your friend like this."

"That's right, Harvey, and I know you think I'm ridiculous coming in here like this, Burt." She threw him a knife-life look over her shoulder. "But friends matter. I thought you knew that."

I started to straighten the paper bags on the end of the register counter. "I do know that, Mom. I'm not betraying my friend to believe what the sheriff believes. I'm simply trusting the evidence."

"Poppycock." My mother's worst non-expletive rang through the store. "That woman could not kill a rabid raccoon, much less a person. I like Sheriff Mason, but he's got this one wrong."

"He hasn't arrested her yet, Sharon," my dad said, trying to soothe her.

"Well, he hasn't exonerated her yet either, at least not in the court of public opinion." She stomped back toward the door. "I'm going to go buy another piece of her work right now, to show I stand in solidarity with her."

If there was one thing I loved deeply about my mother, she was passionate about what she believed, and she'd stand by her beliefs come hell or high water.

"I'm sure she'll appreciate that, Mom," I said.

Mom turned back to me. "Maybe you should consider doing the same, Harvey, *after* you reexamine your loyalties."

My dad gave a little wave as he followed my mom out of the shop.

I leaned back against the half-wall behind the register and laughed.

"Your mom does put on a good show, Harvey," Rocky said from the café behind me. "She's right, though. Henri didn't do this."

I almost turned around and said, "I know," but I caught myself just in time. Instead, I turned slowly and said, "I hope you're right."

Rocky gave me a sad smile and turned to rinse out a coffee carafe.

Gracious, I hated this. But I hated a murderer going free more, and as much as I disliked Wilma Painter, she did deserve justice.

AT NOON, Ollie arrived with two canvases as big as his body held in front of him. I wasn't sure how he'd been able to see to walk up the street, much less bike twenty miles.

But when he leaned them against the bookshelves by the front windows, they seemed to grow even larger. One was a depiction of a tree on a hill, all greens and blues with just the smallest bits of sunshine yellow. It looked like a painting, a lovely landscape, but when I leaned in, I saw it was all pieces of garbage. A spearmint gum package. A label from a can of green beans. The wrapper from a box of baby's rice cereal. The visual effect was striking because the picture had depth and shifted subtly when I looked at it from different angles. Add to that the quiet message of how trash can become beauty, and you had something remarkable.

The second piece was even more three-dimensional. In it, a woman sat in a chair, her stomach exposed between her T-shirt, which was tied in a knot below her chest, and her cut-off shorts. There, just below her navel, was a long, pink scar. The image itself was striking, and I couldn't recall if I'd ever seen an artistic rendering of a woman with a C-section scar before. But what really brought the piece to life was that it was made entirely of sequins. It wasn't garish or glittery though. No, somehow, Ollie had managed to turn those shiny bits of metal into little mirrors that drew me into the image, almost literally, through my reflection. I was in awe, and I decided that if anyone asked me what I wanted for my birthday, I was going to ask for this painting. In fact, I was going to tell everyone I wanted this painting, since I knew they'd probably have to pool resources to get it for me.

Stephen and Walter came in a few moments after Ollie had set up the canvases. I knew as soon as they came in that they loved the work. Stephen's hand flew to his mouth, and he stopped dead in the doorway to stare. Walter moved around him and walked up, silent and gaping.

Meanwhile, Ollie kept his hands in his pockets and tried to look casual. But that shuffling he was doing wasn't the motion of a confident artist. I kind of wanted to hug him.

Fortunately, I didn't have to scare the young man with a surprise hug because my two friends went over and immediately said they loved the pieces. Well, what Stephen said was, "You are brilliant, sir. Brilliant."

Ollie, who I wasn't sure I had ever seen smile, lit up. His whole face changed. He went from a somewhat dour and slightly under-noticeable fellow to a veritable showman. Suddenly, his shoulders were back, and his hands took up animation. But his smile, his smile was what did it. In that minute, I knew that this kid was not capable of killing anyone. I couldn't put my finger on why I knew, I just did.

Walter came over to me. "Harvey, you love these, right?"

"I do, especially that one." I pointed to the image of the woman. "I'm so surprised. I usually avoid sequins fastidiously."

Ollie said, "Most people do. That's the point, kind of. We try to avoid things that make us feel imperfect or draw too much attention to our imperfections. Or we try to cover them up with sparkle."

I looked at the piece again. That was it exactly. The sequins weren't distracting; they were creating. I loved it even more. "Ollie, I would hang that on my wall any day."

"Good," Walter said, "because we're buying both pieces, and we're loaning you the one you love, Harvey, because you need it."

I started to protest, but Walter put his palm up to my face. "You need it, Harvey." I stopped talking.

"You're going to buy them both? But I haven't even told you how much they are." Ollie's nervousness returned. I guessed he was afraid they'd balk at his price.

Walter looked at Stephen. "He's right. We should know the price before committing."

Stephen nodded. "True. What are you asking, Ollie?"

Ollie winced. "Would five hundred a piece be too much? To cover materials. That's all."

Stephen and Walter exchanged a look, and I knew what was coming because I'd seen Stephen do this before, this thing where he makes someone's day in a way they couldn't have imagined before.

Once, in San Francisco, the three of us had been having dinner at North Beach Pizza – their Quattro Formaggi pizza still showed up in my dreams – and a woman pushing a shopping cart came by. She clearly lived on the street, as so many people do in San Francisco, and she was clearly hungry. She'd checked every trash can on the block, and despite the tradition of leaving leftover boxes on the trashcans for people who needed them, no one had yet left anything out.

Stephen took one look at her, grabbed the remaining four pieces of pizza and the pan and ran after her. As Walter and I watched, he handed her the food and then talked with her for a minute. The next thing we knew, both of them were walking into the restaurant. Walter asked the waitress for another setting, and they proceeded to buy that woman – Sable – anything she wanted. It took a bit of coaxing, but eventually, she had five sodas, all four slices of pizza, a chef's salad, and a slice of cheesecake. Plus, we'd had the privilege of getting to know her. She was a musician, a cellist, and she'd been in school at the San Francisco Conservatory of Music when her husband decided to leave her out of the blue, taking with him everything in their bank accounts. She tried to make do at her minimum wage job at a store in the Sunset District, but within three months, she was out on the street because she couldn't afford her rent. She had to drop out of school, and here she was, two years later, just barely making it through each day.

I have to admit, I was feeling pretty smug that day, feeling pretty good about how generous I'd been to share my table with this woman I didn't know. I even planned to help pay the bill for dinner, something which I normally didn't even attempt anymore since my friends always insisted on treating me. But then, Stephen floored me.

"Sable, would you like to come live with us for a while? No strings but no expenses either. You'd have your own room and bathroom. You could spend time with us or not as you'd like. But if you'd like to live with us, we would like to have you be our roommate."

I looked at Stephen with my mouth wide open, and I thought for sure that Walter would put the kibosh on this idea, for the sake of safety if nothing else. But when I looked at my other friend, he was nodding.

By the time we left that night, Sable had decided to take a risk on two strangers who had shown her a remarkable kindness, and I had learned a huge lesson about what real generosity means. Sable lived with Stephen and Walter for six months, and in that time, she got back into the Conservatory, found a job at a local music studio teaching lessons, and received enough money in loans and grants to cover the rest of her expenses.

Now, five years later, she was the principal cellist with the San Francisco Conservatory. Recently, she texted me a photo of herself on a banner hanging in front of Davies Symphony Hall. I had cried.

So when I heard Ollie name that ridiculously low figure of five hundred each for his amazing works of art, I knew that Stephen and Walter would insist on paying more. But then, Stephen had that look, and I leaned forward. Something big was coming.

Stephen stepped forward, put out his hand, and when Ollie shook it, he said, "Great! Five thousand a piece it is. Also, we have a whole floor in our house that's empty. It's got great natural light and a huge room with a concrete floor that has been sealed. There's a small bathroom and bedroom there, too. We've been trying to figure out what to do with the space, so you'd be doing us a huge favor if you'd live there. Help us feel less guilty about the unused rooms and let us be your patrons as you get your art career established."

Ollie was still shaking Stephen's arm up and down, and I thought maybe he would just keep doing that forever since it didn't seem like he could process what was happening. I stepped forward and put my hand on Ollie's arm. "They're serious, Ollie. They mean it. It would mean less of a ride to work for you, right? And more time to make your art."

It took a couple of minutes but, eventually, Ollie turned to focus on me. Then he looked back at Stephen and Walter who were studying his art again, as if they'd just made the most normal suggestion ever. I loved my friends.

"They're serious?" Ollie said, looking at me again.

"Serious as a crab shack running out of Old Bay."

He leaned over and whispered right in my ear. "I need to say no, right?"

I looked at him seriously and said, "No, you need to say yes . . . if you want to. They're good people, Ollie. They mean what they say, and they are excellent cooks."

That smile broke across his face again. "If I can cook at least twice a week, I'd love to, er, help you out. I just need to be sure I can afford the rent. What are you asking?"

Stephen turned back to us and smiled. "Oh, no rent. Just agree to watch the house when we're on vacation. Does that work?"

Ollie looked at me again. "They're serious?"

"Yep. They're serious."

He took a deep breath. "Okay then. Wow. Alright. Okay."

I smiled at my friends. "So when can he move in?"

"Today if you want. The space is empty. We can get a truck and go get your things whenever you're ready," Walter said.

That energy from before was animating Ollie again. "Oh, I'm ready. I've been living on a friend's couch for four months. I'd love a door."

I sighed. There it was, the thing that Stephen had seen that I hadn't. This boy was suffering, and they could help. I felt tears well in my eyes.

The three of them headed out, both pieces in hand. "We'll drop this one off at your place, Harvey." Walter winked as he went out the door.

Ollie gave me a shy wave as he left. *There goes a young man whose life has just changed*, I thought.

Only then did I notice Marcus standing over by Rocky in the café. He had been scheduled to come in at noon and handle closing, but in the midst of the art and the kindness, I'd totally forgotten.

Now, he leaned over and gave Rocky a kiss on the cheek before coming my way. "Ms. B, you are an amazing person, you know that?"

"What are you talking about? That was all Stephen and Walter."

"Nope, that was you. You invited Ollie in. You told your friends. You are the kind of person who has friends like Stephen and Walter. It was you."

He leaned over and gave me a hug. "Thank you," he said quietly before turning to help the woman who had patiently been waiting to buy her copy of *I Capture the Castle*.

"I'm so sorry to have kept you waiting," I said.

"Oh my, don't apologize. That was just the sort of pick-me-up I needed. It's been a hard week." She set her purse on the counter, and I noticed a brochure for the local funeral home sticking out.

"Goodness, I guess so." I gestured toward the brochure. "Planning a funeral is never a highlight, I expect."

She looked down at the pamphlet. "No. No, probably not. My sister died on Saturday."

I shook my head. "I'm terribly sorry. I can't imagine."

She looked at me. "The worst part. She was murdered."

I felt a wave of shock rush from my feet and out the top of my head. "You're Wilma Painter's sister."

"You knew her?" She looked at me with kindness. "I guess everyone knew Wilma. She wasn't always what you'd call easy. Never had been, not even as a kid."

"Buy you a cup of coffee? I'd love to hear about her. I didn't know her well, just through the bank." I tried to suppress my curiosity and pretend I was just being kind.

Marcus smiled softly. "See, it's all you," he said under his breath. Then he rang up the book.

"I'm Harvey Beckett." I extended my hand across my body as the woman and I walked into the café.

"Renee Forsham. Thanks for this. I don't know anyone here, and while everyone has been kind, such a thing does take a person back, you know?"

"I bet." I took the two mugs of coffee that Rocky had poured when I'd waved two fingers at her with a big smile as we approached. "Thanks, Rocky. You're the best," I said.

She smiled and slid two cinnamon rolls across the counter. "Last two."

"You are too good to me. Thank you."

Renee and I took a table by the window, and I explained that she was about to eat the best cinnamon roll she'd ever tasted. But then I had a horrible thought. "You can eat gluten, right?"

She laughed. "Oh yes. I am so grateful that God has not seen fit to take away the simple pleasure of bread." She picked up the roll and took a bite of the size I could really respect.

"If you feel like sharing," I said after having my own healthy bite, "I'd love to hear more about Wilma, especially about her as a kid."

Renee smiled. "She was, as I said, always a little difficult. This one time, I had left a few of our Barbies out of the dream house. When Wilma got home from school – she was probably six at the time – she had a fit. I was made to sit down and listen to a lecture about the importance of tidiness and about how the Barbies must have felt laying out there in the open all afternoon."

I smiled. "I can kind of picture Wilma doing that."

She laughed. "Did I mention I was the *older* sister?"

I cackled. "She had courage. I'll give her that."

"Yes she did. Did you know that she took the job as the manager of this branch way back in 1988? She was the first woman manager in the chain, and she moved here all the way from our hometown up in Indiana. She didn't know a soul, but she took the opportunity when it came. She worked hard, and she was never afraid to see the fruits of her labor." Her voice had a bit of ice to it, and I thought maybe she was simply trying hard not to get emotional.

I tried to imagine Wilma as a woman in her twenties here in rural, isolated St. Marin's. It couldn't have been easy. "She didn't marry?"

Renee shrugged. "She dated, discreetly, but this town wasn't all that welcoming to lesbians back then."

"Oh, I didn't know," I said, and once again, I realized how very little I knew about the people I saw regularly. "No, I imagine that wouldn't have been easy. Gosh, that seems almost impossible."

"It was hard. But Wilma was determined, and then she came to love it here. She told me stories all the time about the people in this town, about who was having children and who was getting married or divorced. She even told me about you, said that I should come see your "cute little bookstore" when I visited again." She looked down at her hands. "And here I am, on my next visit."

"Goodness." I let the silence hold her grief for a minute before speaking again. "Is there anything I can do? Anything we can do in the shop?"

She looked up and smiled again. "What a kind offer. Mostly, I'm just here to oversee all the processes that Wilma already put in place. She was thorough, and so everything from her funeral to her casket to the interim bank manager is already in place. So no, I don't think there's anything you can do, but thank you for asking." There was that ice in her voice again.

"Anytime. If you think of something, you'll let me know?"

She stood then, shoving the last bite of her cinnamon roll in her mouth, "I will. Thanks for this."

"Anytime. And do be sure you let me know about the services. I'd like to be there, and I expect a lot of the folks in town would. To pay our respects."

"Absolutely. Everyone is welcome, well, everyone except the killer, that is." She looked at me intently. "I hear they've got a suspect in mind."

Again, I was stupefied at how quickly word traveled here, even to visitors. "That's what I hear too."

"Well, if she did this, this Henrietta Johnson woman, she'll get what she deserves." Renee's voice wasn't just edged with ice now. It was a full-on freeze-over, and I shuddered.

Renee adjusted her shoulders and let out a long sigh. "Thank you again, Harvey."

I waved as she went out the door, and then I picked up my phone and called Deputy Dillard. He needed to know that Wilma's sister was in town and that she was not trifling about what should happen to the murderer.

For once, I was glad I wasn't sleuthing.

5

When I was younger, Thursdays had always been my favorite days. I've always been the kind of person for whom the anticipation of the thing almost always matters more than the thing itself, so looking forward to the weekend, especially for me as a bookish, nerdy teenager, was always way better than the weekend.

Now, though, Thursdays didn't stand out as much. I loved how I spent my days, and that was a gift because I'd been dreaming of a bookstore for as long as I could remember. And when you want something this badly for this long, it can really disappoint you. All Booked Up didn't disappoint, though. Not at all.

This Thursday, however, I dreaded, despite the fact that we were having a barbecue at Stephen and Walter's house that night. First, Deputy Dillard was coming into the shop even before we opened to talk about what Renee said. Then, I knew I'd probably have to lie to people, including my parents, and I felt especially guilty about that because we had just started really connecting after several years of pretty intense hostility.

. . .

THIRD, Galen Gilbert was coming in – I wasn't dreading that at all – but he was bringing a photographer to do a shoot of him and some of our books and décor for various publicity purposes. I was super happy Galen had asked if they could use the store, and I really was glad we could do it. But I felt frazzled and tired already, and just the idea of having a photographer moving things around and needing me to get things had me feeling over-whelmed by the time I got my coffee poured.

Still, I was a grown-up, a fact I reminded myself of on the days when I felt like calling in sick and watching *The Good Place* all day, and I could handle it. I ate my two pieces of cheese toast as a treat to myself, gave Aslan a little tuna to treat her, and then leashed up Mayhem for her daily treat of a walk. That girl loved her walks. Sometimes, I wished I had a big old farm where she could run free as she wished, but then I saw her sleeping away the days between our strolls and felt like she might not take advantage of the roaming as much I imagined. She had a good life.

When I reached the store, Rocky had already gotten to the café so she could work on our bi-weekly coffee order, and I was grateful to smell the aroma of fresh brew when I came in. The deputy wasn't due for another fifteen minutes, and so I headed over to the café to get a cup of that goodness. The coffee at home simply was not going to be enough to get me through this day.

Rocky smiled when she saw me, but there was something in her face, a hesitation, that made me think something was on her mind. "Things okay with Marcus?" I asked.

Her smile got wider. "Yes, they're really good actually. He's such a really, truly good person, you know?"

"Well, not like *you* know, but yes, he is." I studied her face for a minute. "You okay?"

"That obvious, huh? I never could lie."

I laughed a bit too hard. "Tell me about it."

Rocky twisted up her mouth and looked at me through squinted eyes. "I don't know. I think you've been doing a pretty good job."

For a moment, I tried to look shocked, horrified, but I was no actress. I sighed and said, "So you know, too?"

"Knew that first day the sheriff came in, and you started talking all loud about how Henri was guilty. You are anything but subtle, Harvey." She tilted her head and smirked.

I rolled my eyes. "The sheriff should have never trusted me with this. I'd be a terrible member of the *21 Jump Street* team."

Rocky laughed. "You know that movie?"

I had to think a minute until I remembered that Tatum Channing, or was it Channing Tatum? – I never could get his names in the right order – was in some remake. "Oh, I was talking about the TV show with Johnny Depp, Dustin Nguyen, and Holly Robinson."

"There was a TV Show? Johnny Depp – he didn't play an undercover narc, did he? He's so old."

"Hey now," I said. "I've had a crush on him for, well, decades."

"You have? We're talking about the same guy, right? Jack Sparrow with the eyes painted on his eyes."

"That's the one. I used to even have a purse with his face on it."

Rocky whipped out her phone. "I have to see some photos of this guy when he was younger. He's just so dad-like."

I groaned and walked back to the register in the bookstore with my coffee.

I had just finished straightening all the money in the cash drawer

– something I never did unless I was nervous – when Deputy Dillard came in. "Hi Officer."

"Hi Harvey. How you doing? Just thought I'd stop by," he shot a glance over to Rocky in the café, "and do a neighborhood check." He was almost as bad an actor as I am.

"Don't bother. She knows."

"Another person knows? Harvey, you are really bad at this."

"Yes, yes, I know. My friends just know me well."

"We sure do," Rocky piped in from behind me.

I turned and stuck my tongue out at her before turning back to Dillard. "They won't tell, though. None of them will."

He nodded. "Well, tell me about this interaction with Renee Forsham. How did that all come about?"

I recounted my conversation with Renee from the previous day and told him that she'd seemed very personable, much more in touch with people's feeling than her sister but that her threat had put me off, made me a little nervous.

"A little suspicious?" Dillard asked.

"Maybe," I said, "but she did seem sincerely grieving, too."

"I've seen murderers grieve. Just because they killed the person they love doesn't mean they don't also miss them."

I shook my head. "I guess. Seems like if you'd miss someone maybe you shouldn't choke them to death, but maybe that's just me."

Dillard smiled. "Well, thanks for this. I'll look into it." He closed his notebook and leaned closer. "Now, we have four suspects. We should be narrowing that pool down, not making it wider."

If I didn't count Henri as the fake suspect, I figured they must be thinking Cynthia and Ariel from the bank, Renee, and Ollie. "Ollie's still a suspect?"

Dillard nodded. "Yep, we haven't been able to place him on the morning of the murder."

"Well, where does he say he was?"

The officer shook his head. "He says he was 'creating art.' Not much of an alibi."

"True, but he is an artist. A really good one." I took out my phone and showed him the pictures I'd taken of the pieces Stephen and Walter had bought.

"Those are good, at least I think so. They're interesting. I don't know much about art." He sighed. "Still, his art can't verify his whereabouts."

I popped my lips. "Right. Well, we'll just have to find the real killer then." I heard my slip as soon as I spoke. "I mean you will. Not me. I'm not sleuthing."

He laughed. "Good. Keep it that way."

GALEN AND MACK, his English Bulldog, came in about eleven-thirty with their photographer, a very tall woman with the most beautiful skin I'd ever seen. It was the color of mahogany and had this glow to it. I couldn't figure out why she wasn't in front of the camera herself until Galen explained that she'd gotten her start in photography as a fashion model. Once again, my mild-mannered friend surprised me with who he knew.

While she scouted out the prime shooting locations, Galen and I caught up. I told him I'd missed him for his usual Tuesday visit, and he explained that he just couldn't make the trip twice. "Too many books to read."

"Ah, if ever there's a reason for staying home that I understand, it's reading. What's your latest?"

He grinned. "The latest Bruno book."

"Ooh, I love those stories. He makes me want to move to Italy but only if I can live in a guest house on his property and have him cook for me."

Galen snickered mischievously. "Are you saying you'd like to be one of Bruno's wonderful lady friends?"

"Well, I'm not saying I'd turn it down." I grinned.

The photographer waved to Galen, and he gave me a wide-eyed stare as he followed after her. "Wish me luck."

Galen was probably in his early sixties, so not exactly the demographic that has taken to social media with the most gusto. But he had over sixty thousand Instagram followers last time I'd checked, and he got thousands of likes, shares, and comments on his photos every day. Mack was a regular highlight of his posts, but it was his bookish sharing as a Bookstagrammer that had garnered him his fame. I had a suspicion that a large part of his following was mystery-loving women because Galen was an avid mystery reader, especially of cozy mysteries, which were typically the purview of older women. He devoured them, and his photos of the book covers were always beautifully done as were his captions. I would follow him, even if I wasn't lucky enough to be his local bookseller.

Plus, he'd been deeply committed to All Booked Up ever since we opened. I knew he wanted to help me out by having his photo shoot in the store. Every time he mentioned the shop, our customer traffic increased, as did our online orders. He was like our very own bookstore leprechaun with his Instagram gold.

As Galen, the photographer, and a reluctant Mack moved through the store, I felt the stress I'd been carrying all day ease.

The conversation with Dillard had been fine. I had to lie to one less person now, and the photoshoot was requiring literally nothing of me. I sat back on the stool behind the counter, took a deep breath, and smiled.

Then, the bell over the door dinged, and my mother blew in. This time, my dad gave her a long lead and their dog Sidecar stayed close to him as they went right to the café while Mom headed straight for me. I had this impulse to throw my arms up in front of my face as she approached.

"I wanted you to know that I commissioned a piece for your bedroom from Henri. It's going to be designed to hang just at the end of your bed so you have to begin and end your day with her on your mind. I can't believe you, Harvey."

I stared at her. If she didn't look so hurt behind all that anger, I might have laughed it off, chalked it up to my mom's dramatics. But she did really look hurt. It had been a big thing to move to this town, to give up life in Baltimore with her volunteering and Dad's business. I wondered if she thought my suspicions of Henri were harming the town she'd just started calling her new home.

Right then, I made a decision. I knew I was going against my word to Tuck, but I couldn't take this anymore. "Mom," I crooked a finger toward myself, asking her to lean in. "I need to tell you something."

She looked at me skeptically, then huffed and moved closer. "You cannot tell anyone this." I glanced back at the café. "Okay, you can tell Dad, but no one else. Got it?"

I could see the glee spreading up my mother's face. She loved a good secret, almost as much as I hated one. "Got it." She placed her hand over mine as if she hadn't just come in here to lambast me and spend money to induce a deep and lingering guilt in my soul.

I sighed. "I don't really believe Henri killed Wilma." I waited as understanding washed over Mom's face.

"You don't?" She went from gleeful to puzzled.

"No. It's part of a ruse that the sheriff set up while he conducted the actual investigation." We were whispering, but I still was concerned someone would over hear. "I'll tell you more later at Stephen and Walter's." And with that statement, I realized I was going to tell all my friends. I just couldn't keep this up.

Mom stepped back and looked at me as if she was evaluating my personhood afresh. "You're something, Harvey Beckett. You're really something."

I was not sure whether "something" constituted a compliment, but since the wild wind of motherly manipulation seemed to have passed, I was content.

"Who knows the truth?" Mom lowered her voice, but I appreciated that she kept her language opaque.

"You, Mart, Daniel, Rocky, and the police. That's all. I'll tell Stephen and Walter tonight."

Mom's hands flew to the top of her head. "Henri doesn't know." Her voice got a bit louder, and I put a finger to my lips.

"Sorry. Yes, yes, Henri, Bear, and Pickle also know. They've been in on it from the beginning."

I just had time to notice the relief on my mom's face when I saw a police car go by and noticed Henri in the backseat. She gave a small wave as she went by.

"Guess the sheriff just upped the game," I said as Mom and I watched the cruiser head up the street.

"Well, you can't very well go to the station to visit since you think she deserves to be there." Mom's voice was back to full volume now. "She doesn't need that kind of bad energy, so I guess I'll just have to go. That's what people do, daughter, when they care about someone. They support them." Then she gave me a *very* exaggerated wink and walked away.

I was pretty sure that woman would never cease to surprise me, and I found myself very glad of that fact.

By THE TIME the store closed that day, I was ready for a bonfire, some good food, friends, and a beer. I normally wasn't a beer drinker, but tonight, a beer and the warm spring air seemed perfect. I texted Stephen to be sure they had some.

"We do, but it's hoppy. I'll grab something you'll like."

Man, my friends were good to me.

"Thanks. See you soon," I responded.

Daniel was just walking up when I locked the front door, and he and I switched leashes. It just worked better if I handled the low, slow Basset, and he managed the tugging beast of a Cur. In moments, the synergy of our relationship almost stole my breath.

It was a beautiful evening for a walk, and if Route 13 had been at all friendly to walkers at night, we probably would have gone that route. But instead, we swung by my house for the pick-up that Daniel had recently gifted me. I'd just gotten it back from the body shop where it been painted the bright aqua that I found so quintessentially vintage, and I thought driving it down the road on a spring night sounded just about perfect.

Because Mayhem – and often Taco – went along on any road trip, Daniel had rigged sturdy safe kennels in the back for them. They were the kind hunters used for their beagles and hounds, but Daniel lined these with faux lambskin, something I did not think any hunter I knew would do.

Mayhem always loved a car ride, but now, I had to practically restrain her when she saw the truck. She loved her kennel so much, and Taco, despite the fact that there was no way he could jump into the truck bed and, thus, had to be hefted in, felt about the same. Once, I had suggested we build Taco steps so he could walk in, and Daniel had needed to take a walk to calm his fit of hysterical laughter. Guess he'd rather lift his dog's eighty pounds of dead weight.

Tonight, the dogs were as eager as ever, and after Mayhem launched herself into the bed and went right into the kennel, Daniel lifted Taco and grunted.

"See? Stairs," I quipped.

"I am not building my dog stairs so he can take a ride in a vehicle. No way." He was smiling when he spoke, but I also knew he was serious. Daniel loved his dogs, but he had his limits.

I started up the engine, and she purred to life. I knew the truck was female, but I hadn't yet thought of a name for her. Everyone else, however, had their own suggestions. Lucas wanted "Her-Story" out of some weird sense of feminism, dedication to history, and my life, but I felt like that wasn't really a name. Walter had suggested Stella, as in Tennessee Williams, but I could only think of the French bulldog on *Modern Family*. Mom thought something straightforward would be best, so Aquamarine was her suggestion.

Ironically, the one person whose idea I wanted to hear didn't believe in naming cars, same as he didn't believe in dog stairs, I guess. But tonight, I thought I'd try him out. "I'm thinking of naming the truck Susie Q."

"Oh, that's cool. It fits. Right vintage." His voice was neutral, attentive but not enthusiastic.

"You don't like it?" I was baiting him, and I knew it.

"Harvey, you know that I don't do car names. But if you want to, that's totally fine. I think Susie Q is great.'

I sighed. "I'll run it by everyone tonight, right after I fess up to lying about thinking Henri was a murderer."

Daniel turned in his seat and looked at me. "You're what?"

"Well, you and Mart already know, and I told Mom today, so Dad knows by now. Rocky figured it out, too. So that just leaves Stephen and Walter to fill in." I sighed. "I just can't do it. I'm such a bad liar, and I hate lying to my friends."

"I hear you, and I get it. But you're forgetting something."

"I am?" I thought he might say something about my promise to Tuck or risking the investigation. But no.

"Cate and Lucas are coming tonight."

I felt a cold wave wash over me. I had totally forgotten about them, which was horrible since I considered Cate one of my closest friends. "Crap. Well, then, I can't tell Stephen and Walter, at least not tonight. I don't want to be whispering and then have to do that thing where we all stop talking if Cate or Lucas walks in."

I stared out at the dusky purple settling into night around the truck. Cate was an amazing person, but she was also a huge personality. One afternoon, when we were at a mall in Delaware, she was in a silly mood, so she got up onto a table and shouted, "May I have your attention, please? May I have your attention?" Gradually, the entire food court went silent as this small woman stood on a wobbly table outside the Panda Express. Then, she looked out, grinned, and said, "Thanks. I just wanted a little attention."

I had wanted to bury myself in fried rice, but the shoppers loved it . . . and Cate loved their adoration.

So if I told her that I didn't think Henri was guilty, especially if I couldn't effectively communicate that this was still a secret, an important secret, I was afraid word would get out, simply because of her massive relief. I sighed.

Across the car, Daniel was very quiet.

"Right? That makes sense, doesn't it? Not to tell them tonight since Cate will be there?"

Still more silence.

"Or are you saying that I shouldn't tell them at all?" I had this tendency to spiral when I thought someone was judging me, especially if that someone was a person I cared a great deal about. Within the span of three seconds, I can decide that they think I'm a horrible person and that they can't believe they ever wanted to spend time with me. "You think I'm making a mistake, don't you?"

Daniel reached across the bench seat and took my hand. "No, Harvey. I think it's good to tell everyone, even if only because it eases your conscience. I was just pondering whether or not you should go ahead and tell Cate and Lucas, too. What if she's hurt that you told all of us but not her?"

He had a point. A good point, but I still couldn't shake my concern about Cate's ability to keep a secret when it would mean less suffering for her friend . . . although Henri was in the know, so maybe if I explained that . . .

I watched the white line on the side of the road begin to shimmer in my headlights, and I took a deep breath. "Okay, tonight. I'll tell everyone."

"Good. I think that's a good choice," Daniel said as he gave my hand a little squeeze.

We rode in silence the rest of the way to Stephen and Walter's amazing house, and with each mile, I felt better, more buoyant. I ran through my mini-speech in my head, and by the time I pulled off the highway into their long drive, I was ready. Once everyone had a bottle of beer or a glass of wine, I'd make my announcement and watch relief pass over Cate's face.

After I parked, Daniel lifted both dogs down to spare their legs, and I grabbed the banana pudding I'd made. Then, we climbed the steps toward the front door and rang the bell.

Everyone was in high spirits, and the large open living space was charged with fun and laughter. Our dogs took off to hunt down Sasquatch and Sidecar, and I headed in to find that beer Stephen had picked up while Daniel got waylaid to talk ball bearings or something with my dad by the door.

I was still running through what I was going to say as I rounded the corner into the kitchen and almost ran into someone. I stepped back and smiled into the face of Cynthia, the bank teller, and my entire speech turned to ash in my mouth.

6

"*Hi* Harvey," Cynthia said with a broad, white smile. Her hair was in twisted braids on top of her head, and she looked wonderful. I would have looked like an aged Heidi of the goat herders.

"Oh, hi Cynthia. Good to see you." I glanced past her toward the six-pack of Starr Hill Love beer that I could see behind her. "Would you mind grabbing me one of those?"

"Definitely. That beer is so good."

I glanced at the Natty Bo can in her hand and smiled.

"This beer is not good. Not at all, but it tastes like home to me, so . . ."

"You're from Baltimore?" National Bohemian Beer was the unofficial beer of Baltimore City. The mascot, Mr. Natty Bo himself with his huge handlebar moustache, stood over the factory and blinked in neon across the city day and night.

"Yep. Grew up in Fells Point, before it was trendy."

I smiled again, at a loss for what to say for the second time in thirty seconds. Cynthia didn't look old enough to have predated the fashionable upswing of Fell's Point, but I didn't think it polite to point that out. "Ah, I do love Fell's Point."

"Me, too." She sighed. "I miss it." Her face flushed, and she flapped her free hand around. "Don't get me wrong. I like it here, too. I just—"

"Believe me, I understand. If you love the city, you just love it. St. Marin's is not a city, and if you want restaurants that say open past nine or a movie theater or more than three blocks of shops, then this is not the town for you." I touched her arm. "I moved here from San Francisco. I get it."

"You left San Francisco to come here?"

I laughed. "I did, and for me, it was the best decision ever. But that doesn't mean this is the right place for everyone. What brought you to St. Marin's?

"My job at the bank. It was a promotion, and I wanted a chance to save some money and maybe travel a bit."

I tucked away that little bit of info to consider later. "Do you like banking?"

She crinkled her nose. "Not particularly. But I'm good with numbers. I got my degree in accounting at Maryland, but I didn't take the CPA exam. I just couldn't bear the pressure. So banking is a better fit." She took a sip of her beer, and I saw her eyes scan the room. "Maybe it'll be easier now," she said quietly.

"Ah, yes, I imagine Wilma was hard to work with."

"You have no idea. That woman would come in angry and start finding things to complain about – ink pens at the counters not tied down with those little silver ball strings, name plates not parallel to the front of the counter, someone's hemline a little too short. By the time we opened, most of us just wanted to go back home."

I nodded and sipped my beer. One thing I knew was that when people felt like they had someone who would listen, they would often unload a lot, maybe more than they intended to.

"This one day," Cynthia continued, "Ariel was talking with a customer, and Wilma walked in, grabbed her by the arm, and literally dragged her into the lobby to berate her about her perfume. Wilma got headaches from perfume, and Ariel must have forgotten." Another sip from her beer. "I thought Ariel might cry right there, but she held it together enough to finalize the loan paperwork. But later, I heard her crying in the bathroom."

Cynthia stopped and looked at me with embarrassment. "I'm so sorry. I don't know why I just told you all that. You're here to have fun with your friends, not hear about my work problems. And anyway, the problems will be done now, I hope."

I gave her a small smile. "Why didn't you quit?"

A flush of color passed up Cynthia's neck, and she looked over my shoulder. When I turned to see what she was looking at, I saw Deputy Dillard, and he had the same rosy cheeks as Cynthia.

I raised my chin and said, "I see you two know each other." But I might as well have tried to communicate with them telepathically because they didn't even glance at me. "Well, then, Cynthia, it was nice talking with you. Good to see you, Deputy." I stared at them a second longer to see if they might snap out of their mutual admiration and respond, but nope. I headed off to find Daniel.

He was still trapped with my dad, and when I sidled up and put my arm around him, he squeezed my shoulders really tight in the universal signal of "Get me out of here." I looked at my dad and said, "Dad, Mart is thinking of investing in the winery. I think she could use your advice." I looked over and caught the eye of my best friend who was standing in the doorway to the deck and mouthed, "I'm so sorry," as my dad headed her way. Dad could not pass up a chance to give someone business advice. I just hoped Mart would forgive me.

I tugged Daniel into the alcove by the staircase and said, "Cynthia from the bank is here. I don't think I can tell everyone the truth just in case she's the murderer. Plus, Deputy Dillard is here. He wouldn't take kindly to me blowing the plan."

"Ugh," Daniel slumped against the wall. "I was looking forward to not having to avoid the topic, too."

I stretched up and kissed him. "I know. This is hard for all of us. I'm sorry."

He gave me a tight hug just as the front door opened beside us and the sheriff and Luisa walked in. I was pretty sure that she was carrying a tray of tamales, and I could feel my salivary glands come to life.

"Hi," I said as I hugged them both and then got right to business. "Are those your tamales?"

"To grill over the bonfire. Walter wanted to try it."

"That is amazing," I said and was again glad that I'd chosen beer for the night.

"Have you seen him?" Lu asked.

I scanned the room again. "Yep, over there by the grill."

"I'm going to take these out, Hon," she said to Tuck over her shoulder. "Daniel, can you help me? I don't know if I can do the deck stairs in these heels." Her orange spikes definitely required some assistance.

Daniel gave me a kiss on the cheek and then took the tray from Lu, leaving the sheriff and me standing in the foyer.

"Harvey, I was hoping I'd find you here. How you been?"

I put on my best "Good, good, how about you?" face and said, "Eh, I hate lying."

He nodded. "I know, but good news. We don't have to lie anymore."

"You caught the murderer?"

"No, not yet, but the diversion helped, and I think we'll soon have the evidence we need." He looked across at our gathered friends and I saw his eyes rest on Dillard and Cynthia. He frowned.

"Those two are kind of too blonde and perfect for each other don't you think?" I asked with a smile.

"Excuse me," he said and headed for the kitchen.

I am a terrible person, so I walked right behind him, acting like I needed another beer. Mine was still two-thirds full. I was a slow drinker.

From my not-so-surreptitious position beside the fridge, I heard Tuck say, "Dillard, may I have a word?"

The deputy's face turned a deep red as he apologized to Cynthia and followed the sheriff to the deck. Guilt raging but not slowing me down, I went as quickly as I could to the basement stairs, my second beer forgotten, where I knew I could step out on a patio below the deck to eavesdrop further.

It was only when I threw open the door at the bottom of the steps that I remembered Ollie was living there. Okay, it was only when I saw the easels, TV, and futon with Ollie on it that I remembered. Talk about embarrassing.

But I tried to play it off. "Hi Ollie. Didn't see you at the barbecue and wanted to say hi." I tried to look really friendly, especially since I'd just burst into his apartment without even knocking. "How are you?"

Ollie, to his credit, either hid any negativity about my disrespect for his privacy or didn't have any because he just stood up and gave a small wave. "Hi Ms. B." He stretched an arm out beside him. "Welcome to my humble abode." Then, he gave me a smile.

I smiled back and dropped to the futon beside him with an oomph. Those things are low to the ground. He was watching something I recognized, but I couldn't quite place it. So I turned toward him instead. "How are you liking it here?"

He looked around the room. "It's amazing. I can't believe they are letting me live here for free."

"Yep. They're pretty amazing." I watched the TV for a few more seconds, trying to place the movie. "You know, you could come upstairs?"

"Oh, I know," he said. "Stephen and Walter invited me. But sometimes, well, sometimes I just need to be by myself. I get time with people a lot at work."

I could so relate to that. "I get it." I followed his gaze back to the TV and when I saw a young Jason Alexander, I finally realized he was watching one of my all-time favorite movies. Anytime I need to be reminded of good in the world, I watched this film. "Wait, you're watching *Love! Valour! Compassion!?* I love this movie."

He sat forward and looked from me to the screen. "Me, too. They're all just such good friends." His voice was quiet and a bit sad.

"Yeah, they are." I thought about my life at his age, about how I'd left most of my good friends from college as we set out on our own paths and how lonely I'd been. It had taken me until my late thirties to find good people, and it was only here, now, that I felt I had friends like those in the movie. "You'll find your lake people, Ollie. You will."

He gave me a small smile and turned back to the screen. "I hope so."

I patted his shoulder and then pried myself up and out of the futon. "Thanks for letting me stop by."

Without looking away from the movie, he said, "You can go out the back door if you want to slip down to the water for some quiet time."

I chuckled. He'd known all along that I was headed out that way. "Thanks." I walked carefully around the easels by the door, averting my eyes in case he didn't want me to see his works in progress, and opened the French doors onto the patio.

As soon as I stepped out, I could hear Tuck's voice. It was quiet, but very intense. "You understand, Dillard? This cannot continue."

There was a moment of silence, and then I heard footsteps. I'd missed the good part, but part of me was relieved. If lying to my friends was bad, eavesdropping was somehow worse, and yet, here I was.

I looked out over the creek behind my friends' house and took a deep breath. Here, this close to the bay, even fresh water scented the air with salt, and while I was not a beach person in the suntan-lotion-and-wave-diving sense, I did love that smell. It soothed me.

I decided to walk out onto the lawn and stroll. That alone time Ollie had mentioned sounded pretty great. But as soon as I walked out from beneath the deck, Tuck called to me. I turned and did my best to act surprised to see him there. "Oh, hey

Tuck." I knew I didn't sound convincing, but he must have been too distracted by his conversation with Dillard to notice.

"I just got a text from Henri. She and Bear are on their way, so I'm going to let everybody know she's cleared. Thought you might want to be in here for that." He gave me a forced smile.

"Definitely. I'm on my way." Stephen and Walter had become good friends with Henri and Bear because of their shared love of art, so I wasn't surprised they were coming, especially since my friends had not for one second thought she was capable of murder. Oh, it was going to feel good to come clean.

This time I walked up the stairs beside the house and came back in the front door. Daniel did a quick double-take from where he stood by the sofa, and I gave him a wink before I slid in next to him.

I was particularly eager to hear whether or not the sheriff would announce that his investigation of Henri had been a complete ruse.

"Friends, I've asked our hosts if I can make a quick announcement. Henri and Bear Johnson are on their way over, and before it got all awkward in here because I'm here and they are, too," he smiled, and a nervous chuckle passed through my friends, "I wanted you to know that Henri is not the person who murdered Wilma Painter."

It felt like the whole room sighed, and I looked at Cate over by the deck in time to see relief cross her face like a wave of fresh air. She glanced at me then, and I winced. Her stare was still icy.

Tuck must have caught the glare because I saw him follow Cate's gaze to me, and a flash of understanding settled onto his features. "It's best that everyone here know," he flicked his eyes to Cynthia, "that Henri was never actually a suspect. I recruited Harvey to keep up that story while we investigated other leads.

It was our hope that this fiction would bring us to justice sooner."

I risked a glance back at Cate, and she still looked angry.

"Please put all blame for this situation firmly on my shoulders," Tuck continued. "It was a risky move in terms of police procedure, but it was an even bigger risk for Harvey." He raised his Sierra Nevada Pale Ale. "Now, a toast of thanks to Harvey for being a good sport."

I felt very awkward now, but as I looked around the room, I saw my parents and Stephen and Walter grinning with their glasses and bottles in the air, and Daniel gave me a little side hug. Mart whistled, and even Lucas was smiling. Only Cate still glowered.

The relief of having the truth in the air made me a little giddy, but despite the fact that I knew I couldn't control Cate's reaction to this news – or anything, in fact – I still felt responsible. Responsible and sad.

I made my way across the living room to her, and I took her decision to actually let me get there as a good sign. At least I hoped it was a good sign. "I'm sorry," I said.

She nodded. "Why did you do it?"

This was not the question I expected. "To catch Wilma's killer."

"Yeah, I know that, but why Henri? How do you think it made her feel?"

I smiled, and Cate's scowl deepened. "Oh, Henri knew, Cate. From before I did, Henri knew. She was in on the plan."

Cate tilted her head. "She was?"

"Yep. I wouldn't have agreed if she wasn't. I'm not cruel, Cate." I studied her face, and she still didn't look happy. "I thought you'd be thrilled."

She looked away from me, then, out over the deck. "I know I should be, but well . . ."

When she met my eyes again, there were tears in them. "I just wish you could have told me."

"Oh, Cate." I grabbed her in a tight hug, her dark hair tickling my chin. "I wanted to, and if you'd talked to me yourself, you might have figured out I was lying. Everyone else did, but given that you saw Henri every day, it was especially important that you believe she was under investigation. We did it to protect you and her, actually."

A warm pair of arms wrapped around the two us. "I'm sorry, Cate," Henri said. "I know this is hard."

We stood in that tight hug for a few more moments, and then as we stepped back, I realized we were all crying now. Mart joined us, and the four of us formed a circle with our arms around each other's waists. "Friends?" Henri said.

"Always," Cate answered, leaning against Henri's shoulder. "I understand. I guess I just feel a little left out."

I hadn't even thought about that, that she was the only one of us who didn't know. I would have felt left out, too.

"Well, maybe I can feel you let in again. I have news."

Mart rolled her eyes. "Sleuthing news."

"Actually no. Just life in St. Marin's news." I said as I pointed to the guest bedroom just behind Henri. "In there, I'll catch you up."

I caught my mom's eye as we slipped through the bedroom door, and she followed us in. "Is this a girls' gathering?" Mom asked as she climbed up onto the bed with the rest of us.

"Yep, just us five," I said.

"The Chanel girls," Mom replied.

"Huh?" Mart said.

"Like the perfume." Henri answered. "I like it."

I smiled. My mom always had high-end taste. "Okay, Chanel Girls, here's the scoop." I caught them up on what I'd learned from Cynthia about the bank's toxic atmosphere and also about Dillard and Cynthia's, well, whatever it was. I told them about Tuck dressing Dillard down, and then I ended with the piece de resistance, Renee Forsham's threat against Henri.

"Oh my goodness, Henri," Cate exclaimed. "You might be in danger."

Henri shrugged. "Maybe. But let her come at me. These booties are good for some tail-whoopin'." She kicked up her leg and showed off her adorable suede shoes.

"Go get 'em, girl," Mom said, and I cringed. My mom loved her out of date aphorisms.

"So you think it's Cynthia?" Mart asked.

"I don't know. She seems like a sweet girl, but she is also pretty miserable here. Still, I wonder if Ariel might not be a better suspect?" I made myself comfy against the headboard.

"Seriously, anyone named after a Disney princess cannot be trusted." Cate said with a smirk.

I snorted with laughter. "Cate Cho!" I tried to sound scolding but I couldn't stop laughing long enough.

Just then, there was a knock at the door, and Walter popped his head in. "Ladies, I hate to break up this adorable gathering before the pillow fight starts, but we're ready to eat."

I grabbed a throw pillow from the bed and tossed it at the door just as my friends did the same. Walter rolled his eyes but then gave us a big grin.

"We'll be right out," I said. As we stood, I turned to my friends, "Now, not a word of this. The police know all this, but no need to give away their leads."

Mom put her hand out, palm down. "Agreed. Hands in, ladies."

We all put our hands in, one on top of each other. "One, two, three – Chanel," Mom prompted.

"One, two, three – Chanel," we said in unison. I never would have imagined I'd do a huddle around a perfume with four women I adored, but I was feeling great when we went back out for those enchiladas.

I spent the rest of the evening moving from person to person, talking with my friends, and enjoying the bonfire down by the river. Eventually Ollie made it upstairs and sat with Marcus and Rocky on the deck. I heard a good deal of laughter from their table.

The tamales were so good that I almost didn't save room for one of Lucas's cupcakes, but thank goodness cupcakes are squishy. By the time Daniel and I went to leave about eleven, I was tired, overfull, and completely content.

As I started up the truck and waited for Daniel to settle Mayhem and Taco into their crates, I rested my head against the back of my seat. The men in *Love! Valour! Compassion!* had nothing on me.

FRIDAYS WERE a bit manic now that the tourist season had started. Rocky and I always came in early to do an extra bit of prep – more coffee brewed, more bestselling titles stocked, etc. – and when we opened the doors at ten, we always had people waiting, mostly for coffee but sometimes for their long weekend reading choices.

I loved that – anyone who would wait on a sidewalk for a book got my best attention. One woman wanted something light but also meaningful, and I was thrilled to recommend *Operating Instructions* by Anne Lamott, especially since she had a toddler in tow. An older man asked for something Southern in his thick New Jersey accent, and I handed him a copy of Tony Horwitz's *Confederates in the Attic.* This book recommendation thing was my favorite part of the job, by far.

By the time Marcus came in at eleven, I was pretty sure we'd already beat our Friday record in sales, and I gave a quiet word of thanks for tourism. "It's going to be a busy one," I said as he came to take over at the register so I could get a quick bathroom break.

"The best kind," he said. "By the way, good news about Henri, you stealthy woman you." He began ringing up the sizable stack of picture books a young woman was buying as her young son kept adding to the pile with frequent returns to the children's section.

"I can't believe Rocky didn't tell you."

"Oh, she's a trustworthy one, that woman." He grinned so wide I saw his ears move.

"Yes, yes she is. I hear some people even trust her with their hearts." I gave him a smack on the back and headed for the bathroom.

ON THE WAY to the bathroom, I stopped to tidy up the children's section after our voracious reader's heartfelt, if slightly sloppy, book selection process when someone caught me by the arm.

I turned and saw Ariel, and she looked either furious or terrified.
It was hard to tell. "Can I talk to you for a minute?" she asked in
a voice that said afraid, not angry.

I gazed longingly at the bathroom for a second before saying,
"Of course. Are you okay?" She looked pale, paler than her naturally very fair skin, and her freckles were bright.

Her eyes darted around the store, like she was looking for someone, or hoping someone wasn't there.

"You want to go somewhere more, um, private?" I felt like only
skeezy dudes in B-movies said things like that, but she nodded
quickly, and we headed to the back room. Once again I had the
passing thought that it would be wise to make this an actual
meeting room given how many semi-clandestine meetings I had
in here.

"Ariel, are you okay?" I was growing more concerned by the
minute because now not only was she pale, she was shaking.

She sat down heavily on a big box and put her head between her
knees. Her voice was muffled when she said, "Yeah, I think so.
Yeah. Yeah, I'm okay." A moment later, she sat up and looked at
me. The color had started to come back to her face, and I felt a
breath of relief.

"What's going on?"

"I heard they don't think it's that woman from the co-op who
murdered Ms. Painter." Her voice was quiet, shy almost.

"That's right. The police have cleared her." I had about forty
million questions, but I was going to try out Mom's tried and
true silence technique and not say more than necessary to keep
the conversation going.

"Okay, okay. So then, it's probably what I thought. Okay, Okay."
She was looking at her hands now, not really talking to me.

I sat down next to her and started rubbing small circles on her back. The woman was clearly upset, and comfort, however small, was always a kindness.

She took a deep breath and asked, "Do you think they'll look at bank employees next?"

I tried not to react to this question because, well, yes, it must have been obvious to most everyone that if someone at the co-op hadn't been taking the money then maybe someone at the bank was. "I'm not sure. I don't know the details. Why do you ask?" And *why are you asking me*? I wanted to add.

Her head dropped between her knees again, and I heard her taking whistling breaths through her lips. "It's okay. It's okay."

"It is okay, Ariel. What can I help you with?"

I felt her shoulders begin to bounce, and when I leaned down to peek at her face, I saw tears falling to the concrete floor. I pulled her to me and let her cry.

When it felt like she'd settled, she took a long, slow breath. "I'm sorry. I didn't know where else to go." She wiped her eyes with the back of her hand. "You must think I'm such a mess."

"No, I think you're something carrying something heavy. If I can help, I will."

She sighed and said to the blank wall in front of us, "I'm living in the bank." Then, her eyes darted to mine. "But not in the part where the vault is. In the attic. I climb up there at night before the alarm is set and just stay there until morning. There are sensors and stuff, so I can't come down. I'm not trying to rob anything or anything." She was talking so fast I thought she might pass out.

"Okay. Well, that sounds hard." I said the first thing that came to mind. "I mean being locked up in there from five each night until the next morning, and what do you do on weekends?"

Her eyes were huge when she looked at me. "It is hard. So hard. Now that it's warmer, sometimes I sleep out in the park by the museum. It's quiet, and I can hear the water. That's what I do on weekends when I don't stay with Cynthia."

I felt tears stinging the back of my eyes, but I knew this woman didn't need my pity. "And you're afraid someone is going to find out and think you killed Wilma because she knew."

She nodded frantically. "But I didn't. I didn't kill her."

I took a long, slow breath. "Okay, so then the best thing to do – and I know this is going to sound terrible – is to tell the sheriff what's been going on."

The low keen that came out of her throat sounded somewhere between a whimper and a whistle, and I quickly put my hands on her knees to calm her. "I'll go with you. I know the sheriff. I trust him. He won't tell anyone about this unless necessary, and since you didn't kill Ms. Painter, it won't be necessary, right?"

She slowly nodded her head. "But it's trespassing. He might arrest me."

She wasn't wrong, but somehow, I couldn't see Tuck arresting a young woman for being homeless because, honestly, that's what this was. Another case of homelessness right here in St. Marin's. First Ollie, now Ariel.

"I don't think that will happen. I do think, though, that he might be able to help us find you a place to live." I was actually already considering an option about that, but I had to talk with some folks first before I offered that up. "We can go now if you want. Get it over with."

If anything, she looked more terrified than when she came in, but she nodded. "I don't know what else to do."

"I think you were right to find help, Ariel. It would definitely be worse if it was discovered during the investigation." I stood up and offered a hand to help her to her feet. She took it and didn't let go.

I gave another longing glance toward the bathroom on our way out, and as I stopped to grab my purse at the register, I told Marcus that I was getting an early lunch. Ariel had let go of my hand, but she followed me right to the counter. Marcus was as perceptive as they come, though, and gave me a small nod followed by, "Have a good one, Ms. B. I've got this."

Like everything in St. Marin's, the sheriff's station was within walking distance, just a little off Main Street on the South end of town. It was a lovely day out, low seventies and sunny, so the fact that my truck was back at the house didn't matter. Ariel and I strolled down Main Street, Mayhem ahead of us actually not tugging. She did always know when I needed her best behavior. I was hoping that the stroll would both calm Ariel's nerves and give me a chance to learn a bit more.

"Forgive me, Ariel, if I'm being nosy, but I want to be sure I understand. How long have you been living in the bank?"

She glanced at me before looking straight ahead. "Since February."

Three months then. "That's a long time. You must be a very quiet person."

She smiled at that. "Believe it or not, it was kind of nice. The quiet was peaceful, unlike at home. My brother was in a band, and they were hella loud."

"You have a brother?"

She smiled again. "Yep, he's twenty-one, four years younger than I am. But we were super close until—" She stopped talking.

"Until?"

I heard a catch in her voice when she said, "Until my parents kicked me out."

"Oh," I said. "Was it one of those, we want you to get your feet under you things? Or something else?" I asked out of genuine curiosity but also concern.

"Oh, they would have been happy to have me stay at home forever. They loved that my brother and I were still there . . . I guess they thought of our family as the most important thing in their lives."

Something about the way she said that made me think this wasn't about priorities, like putting your family first. "So, then, why kick you out?"

"I got pregnant." Her voice was monotone.

I stopped walking, but she kept going. Clearly I was missing something. She'd just said she was in her mid-twenties and had gotten pregnant. I had a forty more questions now.

Ariel was a few dozen steps ahead of me when Mayhem and I jogged to catch up. "They weren't happy you were pregnant and not married." My brain finally caught up, too.

"Right. We are, well, they are, pretty religious, and it didn't matter to them that Julian and I had been together for years and that we were going to get married." She choked up then. "It didn't matter to him either, I guess."

"Ariel, he left you when he found out you were pregnant?"

She nodded, and I could tell she was trying hard not to cry again.

"I had nowhere to go, so I took this job here in St. Marin's and hoped I'd be able to get my feet under me and find a cheap place to live for the baby and me . . . then, for just me."

When she took a breath, I said, "Oh, Ariel, I'm sorry." I paused and took a deep breath. If she didn't want to talk about the baby, I wouldn't push. "There are not many safe, cheap places to live here. Believe me I know." Mart and I had considered renting an apartment while we got established here, but it quickly became clear that buying a house – since we had the down payment – was the smarter move for the sake of both our finances and our comfort.

She looked at me then. "Exactly. I tried to save, but I just couldn't afford everything – clothes for the new job, food, the deposit and renter's insurance. Plus, I have student loans. My salary is good, and I have benefits. But my parents kept the car they'd bought me, so I didn't have a way to get anywhere that I had to drive and couldn't afford insurance even if I'd been able to buy a used car . . ."

I stopped her then. "You don't have to explain it to me, Ariel. I know how expensive it can be to be out on your own." I thought of all the times in San Francisco that I'd just wanted to buy one of those fancy Starbucks drinks for a little treat on a Friday afternoon but couldn't because I only had four dollars to make it until pay day.

We'd reached the police station by then, but before we went in, I needed Ariel to understand something. "No matter what happens in here, Ariel, you are not alone. You understand that, right? I am here. I will still be here at the end of this conversation."

Tears welled in her eyes again, and we walked in the door.

*a*s I expected, Tuck was amazingly kind. He hadn't asked any questions when I told him that Ariel and I needed to talk to him in private. Then, when she'd told him about her current residence, the only thing he'd said was, "I understand. Sounds to me like you had every reason not to kill Ms. Painter since a new manager might have meant new procedures that would risk your secret."

At those words, I could see the relief cross Ariel's face.

The police business out of the way, I asked Tuck if there was any way we could get into the bank today to get Ariel's things since she was going to be staying the night with Mart and me. She had tried to protest, but I had shushed her. "Just for a couple of days. I have a plan for something more permanent, okay?"

She just seemed so relieved by letting out her secret that she didn't protest further. I knew what it was to keep a much smaller secret, and so I couldn't imagine how good it felt to not have to carry this huge one for so many months.

Tuck made a phone call to the temporary branch manager, and he agreed to meet Tuck at the bank in an hour. "I have reason to inspect your attic," was all he said on the phone, and I admired him all the more for his discretion.

By mid-afternoon, Ariel was settled into our guest room. Mart had agreed the second I'd called her from the bathroom at the station. (I had taken advantage of the facilities when Harriet had taken Ariel into the breakroom for a coffee and some of the ever-present cookies that Lu made for the officers.) "I can't believe that all these young people are homeless," Mart said. "So awful."

"I agree. But we know that finding an affordable place to rent can be almost impossible. Remember that one apartment you had in San Francisco, the one with the burger place below it that vented its grill right into your bathroom?"

"Oh the smells," Mart had gagged. "It was so bad. But it was cheap."

"Exactly."

I left Ariel on the couch with Aslan, the remote control, and a stack of fresh towels. I had no idea how she had showered – maybe at Cynthia's – but I knew that if I'd been living in an attic and a park for months I'd just really want clean linens, some mindless TV, and hot water.

A small part of me worried that I was maybe being naïve, trusting this woman I barely knew in my house, but the larger part of me preferred to be trusting and deal with the conse-quences if someone broke that trust than to walk around suspi-cious of everyone I met.

Back at the shop, Marcus, of course, had everything well under control, so I texted my friends and asked them to meet me at the shop at seven. "We need a plan," I wrote but then quickly followed up with, "And no, this isn't sleuthing."

I didn't explain via text because I didn't want to risk the message being accidentally forwarded to anyone. I knew my friends would come if they could. Then, I spent the rest of the afternoon, between customers, searching out housing options in the area. I found only three that I thought would work.

By seven, Stephen and Walter, Mom and Dad, Josie, Woody, Pickle, Bear and Henri, Elle, Cate and Lucas, Tuck and Luisa, and Daniel had joined Marcus, Rocky, and me in the café with Mart on FaceTime from her consulting gig in Virginia. Everyone had brought food for our usual Friday night feast, and so we ate while I caught them up on Ariel's situation. Before I even had time to ask, they were brainstorming.

An hour later, we had a plan, and it involved Elle's farm, a whole lot of flowers, and the help of our favorite customer, Galen, and his Instagram followers. I was excited, and exhausted, so when Tuck asked to speak to me as everyone headed home, I almost groaned.

As usual, I telegraphed my feelings right through my face, so Tuck said, "I know. It's been a long day. This is a good thing, Harvey. But we still need to be careful. There's a killer out there, remember?"

I actually had almost forgotten for once in the past week, but there was Wilma's face in the park, and I knew he was right. "I know you don't want to tell me, but are there persons of interest?"

Tuck laughed. 'You and your police TV speak. Yes, and I may actually need your help with that. But not yet. Just be wise, Harvey. Be wise."

I tried to focus on his admonition to be wise, but mostly I just kept replaying the idea that he might need my help again. Nothing made me happier than to be helpful, which sounded altruistic to most people. But sometimes, for me, helping was just about making myself feel valuable. It was a trait I constantly needed to watch in myself.

And yet, I couldn't help but get excited about what role I just might have to play.

SATURDAY MORNING, bright and early, Daniel and I drove out to Elle's farm. Marcus covered the shop on Saturday mornings, so I didn't need to worry about rushing in. But I still had work to do for our big plan. The night before, we'd decided we would hold an old-fashioned "Secret Admirer" Flower Sale. We'd done them in high school with red roses at Valentine's Day, and it was always a popularity contest masked as a fundraiser for the cheerleading squad. I hated that stupid sale.

But we had agreed this one would be different. For our fundraiser to cover Ariel's deposit and first month's rent, we wanted to encourage people to send flowers to anyone they wanted to thank or show appreciation for. Romance was definitely one possibility, but so was gratitude or apology or just downright kindness. We were calling it the "Love, St. Marin's Flower Exchange," and we hoped that people from the community, and visitors, too, might participate.

The way it would work was simple. People would come to any of the participating Main Street businesses – Cate and Henri were talking to the merchants – and purchase a flower to be delivered the next day to anyone within town limits. They'd have the option to attach a small note if they liked, or they could simply send the flower. Elle was giving us the flowers at cost, so at the sale price of five dollars a flower, we'd have the twenty-two hundred dollars we needed for Ariel if we sold five hundred and fifty stems.

The hope, though, was to raise far more than that and be able to start a fund that would assist people out of homelessness in the area. Mom, Dad, and Pickle were meeting with the mayor and the president of the chamber of commerce to see how that fund might be managed and administered. I had no doubt they'd have a plan by the end of the day, and I also suspected that Mom would gladly manage the fund if offered the chance. It was the kind of thing she excelled at.

The apartment we'd settled on was a few miles out of town in a very small apartment complex that was on our one local bus route. Just a one-bedroom in a slightly older building, but the place looked clean and tidy. Josie was going over to check it out today.

With Marcus and Rocky at the shop and Mart off consulting, that left Daniel, two hounds, and me to do the grunt work of harvesting flowers. Despite the fact that Elle and I had become good friends over the past couple of months, I had not yet been out to her farm. So when the truck turned the corner onto her land, I gasped.

Before me were fields and fields of color. It looked like a painting but better. Burgundies and soft pinks, golds and the purpliest purple I'd ever seen. I couldn't believe Elle ever left with this much beauty around her.

I parked the truck, and as we stepped out, Elle came out of the fields, her arms draped in blossoms. Daniel got Mayhem and Taco out of their kennels and brought them over on their leashes. "The yard is fenced, so feel free to let them explore in there," Elle said with a toss of her head over to her adorable farm house behind the fields. "I put fresh water out for them."

"Thanks," Daniel said and headed that way.

I was still standing and gaping at the flowers. Elle followed my gaze and said, "It's something, isn't it?"

I tore my eyes from the flowers and looked at my friend. "It really is. You do all this? Alone?"

"Well, not completely alone. I hire help for planting and big events, but yeah, mostly. It keeps me young," she said with a smile that crinkled the tanned skin by her eyes.

"I'll say." I took a deep breath. "Okay, what can I do?"

"Thought you'd never ask. Follow me." She headed off toward a small, shed-like building at the edge of the closest field. When we stepped inside, the cold pushed me back. It was a refrigerator. "Keeps the flowers longer. We'll harvest what we can today and store them here. I can supplement as we need them, but if we can get the bulk in today, then we start selling and delivering tomorrow, we'll have most of what we need."

I nodded. The plan was to sell one day and then distribute the next with final sales on this coming Wednesday and deliveries on Thursday. If there was one thing I'd learned in my years of work as a fundraiser it was that a deadline drives dollars. Four days would push people to act immediately rather than put it off and then forget. At least that was the hope.

In the cooler, Elle had a tall table that housed a shallow sink. She put the flower stems from her arms into the water and then quickly trimmed their bases at an angle while the tips were submerged before moving them to five-gallon buckets full of water. "They last longer that way," she said.

I learned something new every day.

Back out in the fields, Elle put Daniel and me to work. Our job was to cut tulips and peonies, "the tough girls," Elle called them, and I took that to mean we probably couldn't do much harm. We knelt to the task of gathering a hundred peonies and fifty tulips. Since the tulips probably wouldn't last as long, we didn't want to overharvest for our first day.

Meanwhile, Elle gathered freesia, roses, and sweet peas, outpacing us quickly. Still by the time the air started to warm about nine, we had seven hundred and fifty stems of flowers on hand, and our work – at least our harvesting work – for the day was done.

Elle invited us into her house for some cold iced tea, an offer I was glad to accept, not only because my back was aching from all the bending but because I loved seeing people's homes. The things they displayed always gave me a chance to know them in a new way, and I couldn't wait to see what Elle put out.

I wasn't disappointed either. Her kitchen was made up almost entirely of windows, like a greenhouse, and on each ledge, she had sculptures and geodes, tiny pieces of cross-stitch or framed quotes. It was like walking into the inside of her head. Plus on every flat surface, she had a vase, Mason jar, or shallow bowl with flowers standing or floating. The effect was one of deep welcome and beauty, and I immediately wanted to sit there and sip for hours.

As we all sat silently enjoying the sweetness of Elle's home-brewed iced tea, I looked out over the fields of flowers around us and had a horrifying thought. "Elle, are we wiping out your business? I mean, you do weddings and things. Will you have any flowers to sell?" I was mortified that I hadn't thought of this earlier and terrified that this act that was supposed to be generous was actually going to hurt my friend.

She smiled. "You see how many flowers I have, Harvey. I've already harvested for this weekend's weddings. One of the young women who works for me took those deliveries early this morning. And I didn't give this endeavor more than my business could afford."

I felt relief wash over me and let myself smile again. "Okay, good."

"I'm a business woman, Harvey, same as you. I can only be generous if my business keeps going, so I make sure it does. It's the only way I've been able to keep this up for ten years now."

"Ten years. Wow. That's amazing. I hope I make it to ten." Business at All Booked Up had been good and steady, but I was already worried about the slower months of fall, after the tourist season. I hoped I could keep it up.

Daniel stretched and said, "This is really great, Elle. Thank you."

"My pleasure. I've always said, 'There but for the grace of God . . .'"

I nodded. "I know. Honestly, if Mart hadn't come with me and helped cover expenses the first few months, I might very well have had to live in our storeroom at the shop. I feel so much for Ariel. How awful."

"Yep," Elle said. She took a long sip of her tea, then said, "But here's my question, Harvey. Who killed Wilma? I mean, we don't think Ollie did it anymore, and it doesn't look like Ariel did since that could have put her in an even worse predicament. Obviously, Henri was always a ridiculous suspect," she gave me a long wink, "But who?"

I hadn't really let myself think about it much, but I did wonder. "It almost certainly has to be someone at the bank. Who else would have been able to get rid of the transfer slip but also remove the money from the account, right?"

"Ladies, this feels a bit like stepping into territory we don't need to enter," Daniel said. I could hear the concern in his voice.

"We're just talking," I put my hand on his arm. "No investigating."

"So I suppose the sheriff is looking at all the bank employees, then?" Elle asked.

"I imagine so. But he's keeping a pretty tight rein on the information these days." I sighed.

"As he should," Daniel said and squeezed my hand.

I stood and stretched, wondering how Elle, who probably had a decade on me, did this day in and day out. I felt like I'd need a three-hour massage to be able to move tomorrow. "Thank you, Elle. We better be getting back. After all, these flowers aren't going to sell themselves."

She walked us out, and as we drove away, I kept going back to what Cynthia had said about Wilma's behavior. And I had an idea.

I DIDN'T HAVE a chance to act on my intuition that day, because the bank wasn't open on weekends. Instead, I put myself to work making flyers to hang around town once Cate and Henri reported in on who had agreed to be a point of purchase.

The shop owners on Main Street were amazingly generous folks, and everyone had agreed to participate, even Max Davies, a fact I was both glad about and wary of. Max rarely did things without an ulterior motive, and it seemed that ulterior motive was often getting close to me. Ugh.

By the end of the day, we had flyers up in every participating shop window explaining the sale and identifying the store as a purchase point, and we started getting sales almost immediately, even though we didn't officially start until the next day. The plan was to distribute the previous day's sales at mid-day the next day, so this meant we'd have to start delivering flowers at noon on Sunday. It was going to be a busy day.

Mom, Dad, and Pickle had secured a process for managing the extra funds raised, and as I had expected, Mom was going to administer the fund with Pickle as legal counsel. The money would be in a checking account at the bank, an ironic but not unexpected fact since Wilma Painter's bank was the only one right in town. Dad, Josie, Bear, and Mart would evaluate requests for funds from individuals who needed resources and take recommendations from community members on who might benefit. Given that we had just met two people who were homeless in the last week, this felt like an important and needed resource. I was excited we could create it.

That night, Mart came home from her consulting gig, and she, Ariel, and I had a quiet evening, all of us too tired for much more than Chinese take-out and *Gilmore Girls* reruns. I loved that show with every fiber of my being, especially Jess. Always Jess. More and more, I felt a bit like I lived in Lorelai and Rory's Stars Hollow, and I was not opposed to that idea in any way. I just kept wondering who our Kurt would be.

THE NEXT MORNING when I opened the shop, we had a line of people not only waiting for coffee and books but also to order flowers. I took over twenty-five orders in the first hour I was open, and it became very clear very quickly from the reports I was getting from the other merchants that we'd hit our goal for Ariel by day's end. People loved the idea for its simplicity and sincerity, and the fact that it had a cause behind it gave them even more reason to participate.

About eleven, Elle arrived with her delivery truck full of flowers, and my friends descended on the café to attach the notes to the flower stems with twist ties. I was immediately grateful that we hadn't complicated the process by allowing people to pick the type of flower they wanted to send. It was enough chaos just to get the right notes in the right buckets to go to the right places.

But precisely at noon, everyone but me took off to begin deliveries all around town. It felt amazing to watch this little flurry of flowered buckets head out into the world with words of gratitude attached to them.

Sales continued –of both flowers and books throughout the day – and I was pleased to be able to send a few people down to Elle's farm stand so they could place actual orders for purchase of flowers for their own events. I was a firm believer that generosity was good for business, and this sale was certainly proving that out, and not just for Elle. I'd had a banner day for book sales, too, especially in gardening. Apparently, I wasn't the only one inspired to plant more flowers by the sight of all those blossoms around town.

When we closed up that night, I collapsed into the wingback chair in psychology and let out a soft groan. I felt a bit like Mayhem, who often groaned that way when she lay down, as if the bed freed all the fatigue from her mouth. Daniel was on his way over with a pizza – ham and pineapple on my half, just ham on his, and extra cheese all over. Cate and Lucas had invited us over for dinner, but I begged off, too tired to be social. I just wanted to hang out with my guy, eat grease, and then go home to a hot bath and my own bed. I planned to groan again then.

I'd turned out the open sign and shut off most of the lights in the shop but left the door open so Daniel could get in. When the bell over the door rang, I yelled, "Over here" and put a hand in the air and waved.

To say I was startled when Deputy Dillard stepped around the bookshelf filled with self-help titles would be an understatement. In fact, I shouted at the surprise.

"Oh, I'm sorry, Harvey," he said immediately. "I didn't mean to startle you. I ran into Daniel at the pizza place, and he said you were here. They messed up your order – something about adding green peppers – so they're making him a new one."

I shuddered. "Oh, green peppers make me so sick. Glad they're starting over." I sat up a little straighter in the chair and tried to wake myself up a bit. "What's up?"

"You mind?" Dillard said as he pointed toward the other wingback beside me. "It's been a long day."

"Please, join us." I pointed at Mayhem on the bed between the chairs and was surprised to see her sitting up and alert. She normally barely noticed when people came in. I chalked it up to excitement about the pizza and turned back to the deputy. "Everything okay?"

"Oh yeah. Just wanted to stop in and say how great what you're doing for Ariel is. I can't believe she was living up in the attic above the bank. Incredible."

For a second, I felt protective and upset with the sheriff for telling him, but then I realized her secret was probably part of the investigation now and took a deep breath. "I know. Just the idea of how dark and lonely and cramped it must have been up there. Breaks my heart."

He nodded. "Good thing she had lots to read."

"Amen to that. Books can get you through a lot of hard things." I waved my arm around. "I should know."

He laughed and stood up. "Anyway, just wanted to say thanks." He headed back toward the door but then stopped. "Oh, and good work on not sleuthing, Harvey. You're doing great at keeping your nose clean."

I opened my mouth in a bright smile and said, "Doing my best." I hated being praised for things I didn't want to do.

I collapsed deeper into the chair again and bent down to pet Mayhem. She was still sitting at attention beside me, her gaze intent on the front door.

The bell rang again, and Daniel said, "Piping hot!"

"And without green peppers this time?"

"Dillard found you then?"

I grabbed a slice as soon as Daniel set it on the floor in front of me and placed my leg between Mayhem and the box. "He did. Just wanted to thank us for the flower sale and congratulate me on not snooping."

A soft chuckle passed Daniel's lips. "Bet you loved that."

I smirked and took a bite of hot, greasy goodness.

THE NEXT MORNING I woke early and felt great. I'd slept like a log, a fact I attributed to lots of cheese, a long hot bath, and an eight-thirty bedtime. After I made my coffee and a bowl of cream of wheat, I settled into my reading chair with my latest read, Diana Gabaldon's *Outlander*. I was dying to watch the TV show, mostly for the costumes, and I had a pretty firm rule that if I ever thought I'd read the book I had to read it before the movie or TV version since they rarely lived up to the book. I'd always rather spoil a movie than spoil a read.

I was just into the first racy scene with Jamie Fraser and Claire when I suddenly remembered something that Dillard had said the night before about Ariel reading a lot in the bank's attic. I hadn't thought much of it at the time, given how tired I was and how I'd immediately imagined that's how I'd survive in that situation, but now I realized that Ariel hadn't mentioned that to me at all. If she was a reader, then we had some things to talk about.

She'd been an amazing guest – cleaning the entire house, baking cookies, even weeding my garden beds so I didn't have to. I was going to be sad to see her go, but it looked like the flower sale was going to be quite successful. And if so, then we knew there was an apartment ready for her to move into at the end of the week.

We'd thought about keeping the sale a secret from her, but given the flyers and the buckets of flowers and such, we thought it best to clue her in. She'd cried quietly when Mart and I had shared the news on Saturday night, and when we'd told her that we'd set up the fund so that others wouldn't have to go through what she did, she'd sobbed. The only words I could make out were, "Thank you."

She'd taken it on herself to do a lot of social media campaigning, getting the word out everywhere she could, and I knew that her efforts were working because we were now getting orders through FaceBook Messenger. I hadn't even known you could pay for things through FaceBook.

Between her posts and Galen's regular Instagram stories about the sale, I felt liked we'd covered our online opportunities well.

But this morning, I wanted to talk books, so when she came in the front door, her knees muddy from kneeling to deadhead the marigolds, a little into my reading stint, I popped up. "So I just learned that you're an avid reader? What do you like to read?"

She gave me a puzzled look and said, "I do love to read. Doesn't everybody?"

"I knew we were soul mates," I said. "Favorite genres? Authors? Can you actually pick a favorite book?"

"I am completely incapable of picking a favorite," she said as she filled a giant Maritime Museum mug with coffee. "You?"

"Able when forced but prefer not to." I refilled my cup and sat beside her at the kitchen island. "What would you include in a list of your favorites then?"

We spent the next thirty minutes chatting books. She loved YA fiction, but not so much the fantasy stuff. More things like Michelle Yoon's *Everything, Everything* or John Green. "I'll read anything John Green writes," she said.

"Me, too. Again, soul mates." I put my coffee cup in the dishwasher. "Which reminds me, I need to get his latest book into the store. Remind me?"

"Absolutely." She stood and grabbed the dishcloth to wipe down the counter. "Out of curiosity, how did you know I was a reader?"

"Oh, Deputy Dillard mentioned that you spent your time in the attic reading. I totally would have done the same thing."

She furrowed her brow but then turned back to the sink to wet the cloth and said, "It did make the most of a terrible situation."

I gave her shoulders a hug as I slipped behind her to go get ready for work. "See you at the shop in a bit?"

"Yep, I'm on note and delivery duty today." She turned to me and smiled. "Can't wait!"

THE PACE WAS AS FAST and furious as a Vin Diesel car chase at the shop that morning. Flower purchases were frantic as more and more people heard about the sale, and we had even started getting some straight-up donations to the Fund a Home Fund. Marcus had come up with the name, and I loved it. Mart has pushed for something with a pithy acronym, but none of us were that good with puns. So "Fund a Home Fund" it was.

I had some bookkeeping to do, so Marcus ran the store while I did the accounting over in the café. Rocky's mom, Phoebe, had made a fresh batch of cinnamon rolls to take advantage of the flower foot-traffic, and Rocky didn't even ask before she brought me one. That girl was too good to me.

I was just about done reconciling columns when someone called my name. I looked up to see Cynthia coming toward me. She was cute as always with booties and jeans so skinny that even my legs as a ten-year-old wouldn't have fit in them. Her hair was twisted up in a perfectly messy bun, and I swear her makeup was on so flawlessly that she looked like she wasn't wearing any. Either that or she had the skin of an infant and the rosy glow of a day in a breeze.

I, in contrast, looked a bit like a windstorm had swept my hair into an ocean-like wave, and like I was overtired and over forty, so, like myself, because I was actually not wearing any makeup. We were a study in opposites, Cynthia and I.

"Hey Cynthia. How are you? How are things at the bank?" Their new permanent manager's first day was today, so said the grapevine, and I was dying to know how it was going.

"It's good, I think. The new manager Gabriela seems nice. She wants to make a few changes, good ones but things that take a little work. But she's good."

I smiled. "Glad to hear that. You on break? What brings you in?"

I thought I saw a little fear in her eyes, but before I could be sure, she was grinning and talking. "Actually, I wanted to ask you something." She sat down across from me. "But I don't want to seem nosy. I'm just curious, and I guess a little nervous."

"Sure, what did you want to ask?" I was not unfamiliar with nosiness myself, but unlike Cynthia, I had no shame about just blurting out my question.

"I was just wondering if they had any suspects in Wilma's murder. I know that Henri woman was cleared. But I wondered if they were looking at anyone else?" Her voice was shaky.

"You know, I was kind of wondering the same thing, but no one tells me anything. I'm sure, though, that there's nothing to worry about. Tuck and Deputy Dillard have it under control." I winked at her. "Which reminds me . . . you and Dillard?" Nope, no shame at my nosiness at all.

Cynthia went completely white and began frantically searching her purse for something.

"Oh no, I'm sorry. I've embarrassed you."

She cleared her throat. "It's okay. Just, no, there's nothing going on. I just think he's cute is all. I thought maybe he felt that way, too, but then, well . . ."

I thought about Tuck calling Dillard away and warning him off and immediately felt bad for Cynthia. She'd liked the guy, and he'd probably been forced into giving her the cold shoulder.

"Ugh. Dating is so hard. I hate it. Maybe give him time?" Perhaps when the investigation was over, the conflict of interest for Dillard would go away, I thought.

"Yeah, good idea." She didn't look at me as she stood. "Thanks, Harvey. My break's over, so back to the bank."

She scurried out, and I watched her go, feeling so glad I wasn't in the market for a boyfriend.

$\mathcal{B}$y late Tuesday morning when Galen and Mack made their weekly visit, we had already raised four thousand dollars from the flower sale. Mom had begun a press release campaign for the last day's sale with the hopes we might top seventy-five hundred. Given her enthusiasm – i.e., intense loud-talking and pacing through my shop several times a day – I thought people had probably handed over their cash and thanked people with flowers just to avoid her wrath.

Galen did a video with Marcus about the sale and popped it into his Instagram stories and, within minutes, we had even more donations from all over the country. If Mom's press releases didn't do it, Galen's followers would put us over the top.

On Monday, we'd delivered another five hundred flowers, and this morning before work, Daniel and I had gone over to help Elle harvest again. Mart and Cate had done Monday's harvest shift, and Ariel had offered to go today, but I really wanted to get out there and move my body. Ariel's work in my own garden had meant I hadn't had to do as much physical work as I might have. So this was my chance to burn a few calories and get my muscles moving again. I was ready after the full two days of recovery from the last time.

We'd picked more tulips and peonies, and this time, Elle had let me bring in some sweet peas, too. The beauty of all those blossoms had stayed with me all day.

Now, I was going to take my first and only delivery run because Marcus was in the shop. I had my bucket of flowers – peonies and tulips, the flowers I was coming to think of as my specialty – and my deliveries were right here in town. I'd asked for that circuit so I could personally thank the other merchants for participating, and the flowers I'd purchased for each of them were in my pail, too.

I started at the end of the block with the sewing store where I bought my embroidery floss for my never-finished cross-stitch projects. Then, I moved on down to the stationary shop and the boutique that specialized in clothing made from alpaca fiber. My next stop was Max's restaurant, and I was thrilled to be able to leave his flower with my hopefully innocuous "Thanks, Max" note with his hostess and prayed she followed my instructions to say nothing about who brought it by. I wasn't sure, however, that her knowing wink indicated that she was on my side of this weird thing with her boss.

The guys at the hardware store both blushed when I dropped their tulips off, and Pickle guffawed when I handed him his at his office. "You shouldn't have, Harvey? Matilda will be jealous," he said with a smirk. "I'm going to put it in a vase on the table when we have dinner. It'll make her day to think you thought of me this way." I hadn't yet met Pickle's wife, but she sounded lovely, as lovely as her husband at least.

Finally, I made my way to the bank, where I had flowers for at least six people including Cynthia, Ariel, and the new manager. I was just crossing the street to the front door when I noticed two people in a car in the back of the parking lot. I tried not to be nosy, but I stared just long enough to see it was Cynthia and Dillard . . . and they weren't talking. Nope, that was some serious making out going on.

I smiled to myself as I went in the door. I bet Cynthia was happy now. My next thought was, *I bet Tuck isn't.*

But in all things love, I knew to mind my own business, so I just handed out my flowers, leaving Cynthia's at her teller window, and scooted back out quick as lightning.

Back at the shop, though, I couldn't shake the image of Tuck's face as he saw Dillard and Cynthia together at the barbecue. He was livid, and my friend was not someone to fly off the handle for no reason.

Still, I didn't know what reason he had for being so adamant about Dillard staying away from Cynthia, or at least that's what I surmised Tuck had been telling his deputy on the deck that night. I imagined his concern could be because there was still an open murder investigation going on that involved her boss and, frankly, her, but maybe it was something else. Maybe Dillard wasn't kind to women. Or maybe Cynthia wasn't kind to men.

I eventually got myself so befuddled and frustrated with all my guessing that I decided I need to break my own rule about getting involved with affairs of the heart and texted Tuck. I tried to keep it casual: "Stop by when you can. Have a question for you." But given that I texted him only when in dire need, I imagined I'd see him in moments.

Sure enough, within ten minutes, Sheriff Tucker Mason was in the shop, his Cocker Spaniel, Sandy, with him. "Sandy and I were out for a walk anyway, so we came right over."

I knelt down and gave Sandy's fluffy ears a rub. She did this amazing groan when you rubbed her ears, like she was getting the best massage of her life and didn't care who knew it. It made me happy every time.

"Thanks for coming," I said as I unlatched Sandy from her leash and watched her waddle over to where Mayhem was asleep in the history section. "It's probably nothing, but I thought I should check." I told him what I'd seen in the parking lot, and his face got redder and redder beneath his dark brown skin.

"I see," he said with that tone that signaled he was working hard to keep his temper under control. "When was this?"

I glanced at the clock on the register. "About thirty minutes ago?"

He gave me a curt nod. "Can Sandy stay here for a while?" His words were clipped.

"Of course. As long as you want. I'll take her home with me if you can't make it back before we close for some reason."

"Thanks, Harvey," he said as he stormed out the front door and took a right toward the bank.

A few moments later, he marched past the front of the shop, headed, I assumed, toward the police station. If anything, he looked more angry than ever.

But between the steady stream of customers looking for books – including one woman who was looking for an introduction to personality types to whom I recommended *Reading People* by Anne Bogel – and the flower sales, I lost track of the sheriff and of time. When I finally got a minute to think about Cynthia and Dillard again, it was almost six-thirty, and the rush of the day was finally subsiding.

Marcus stayed at the register, ringing up our last few customers, and I did the rounds, picking up magazines and reshelving titles. I was just coming out of the romance section when the sheriff came back in, and he looked downright exhausted. I pointed toward the fiction section, and he went straight there, dropping into a chair before I even got there. Sandy trotted over, lay her head on his foot, and waited. Dogs know when we need comfort, and what kind. Clearly the sheriff needed quiet companionship, so I took Sandy's lead and simply sat in the other chair next to him.

After a few minutes, he took a long breath and looked at me. "Thanks again for the information, Harvey."

I felt a little guilty about potentially ruining Cynthia's romance, but I also felt like I'd done the right thing. "All sorted then?" I said, trying to be all sly and laid back when really I had seven questions lined up ready to go.

Tuck looked at me out of the corner of his eye and smiled. "It's killing you, isn't it?"

I huffed and collapsed against the chair. "It is. What in the world is going on?"

"You did well, I have to say, to hold out that long given your innate, er, curiosity." His humor was coming back, and I took that as a good sign. "Okay, so Cynthia is a person of interest, as you'd say, in Wilma's murder."

I wasn't surprised to hear that, but still, it made me a little sad. "Okay, got it."

"It's not that we have anything in particular on her. Just that we're looking at everyone at the bank since that seems the most likely person to have access to the co-op's accounts."

"So you do think there's a connection between the thefts from the co-op and Wilma's murder?" I was finally getting some solid information, and I wasn't about to lose momentum now.

"We do. Our working theory is that after her confrontation with Henri, Wilma did a little digging and discovered some anomaly, some digital trail that either told her who the thief was or that made the person think she was on to them at least." The sheriff sighed. "I shouldn't be telling you all this, Harvey, but I'm tired, and you're here. You cannot share this information, okay?"

I nodded, and I wouldn't. I wasn't a good liar, but I was good at keeping confidences. "Dillard was compromising the investigation?"

The sheriff laughed. "There you go with the fake police-speak. Yes, he was creating a massive conflict of interest for himself and the department. Not to mention, if Cynthia is our killer, he's putting himself in a compromising situation as an officer."

"Not to mention as a man. Talk about a Lady Killer." I smiled at my own off-color joke, and the sheriff rolled his eyes. "He's going to break it off?"

"If he wants to keep his job, he is. He wasn't happy about it, but I expect he'll do it."

I sighed. "Poor Cynthia. She really liked him."

The sheriff smiled. "I suspect she'll recover." He stood, and Sandy stood with him, her nub of a tail wagging furiously. "Thanks for watching my girl. The older she gets, the more she wants to be around me."

"With me, it's that the older I get the more I want my girl nearby." I smiled over at Mayhem who was still snoozing amongst the Civil War books. "Have a good night, Tuck."

"You, too, Harvey." He attached Sandy's leash and let her lead him out the door.

I made my way back to the register, where Marcus was just

handling our last customer. "Sheriff Mason looks tired," he said as he came around the counter to lock the front door.

"He does. I think this murder investigation is getting to him. It's got to be hard to not solve it quickly."

Marcus nodded. "I hate unfinished business."

"Me, too!" I said as I pulled the register drawer and began to reconcile it.

We'd had a good day, both in book and flower sales, and I decided to do a night deposit to get the excess cash out of the store and into the bank. I typically just ran the deposits over during the day, but we had a sizable stack of bills in our safe tonight. I knew I'd feel better if I just took care of getting it to the bank tonight.

Marcus and Rocky headed out, locking the door behind them, as I finished up the deposit slip. Daniel would be by any minute to walk me home, and he and I could go by the bank's secure deposit box together.

I had just gotten Mayhem onto her leash when there was a knock at the front door, and I looked out to see a sobbing Cynthia. I tucked the deposit envelope back into the safe, swung the door shut, and went to let the poor girl in.

She collapsed onto my chest as soon as she stepped in the door. "He broke up with me. Why would he break up with me?"

I sighed and led her to the café so that Daniel would see us when he walked up. "Oh, I'm so sorry, Cynthia." And I was.

"He came by today, and things were amazing, like better than ever, but then, tonight he sent me a text saying he couldn't see me anymore." She dropped her face into her hands and cried even harder.

As someone who had lived through a fair number of heartbreaks herself, I had learned that what the "dumpee" wants most of all is a reason, something that makes perfect sense, that frees them from some sense of failure or inadequacy and puts the blame squarely on the dumper. I did my best to both give Cynthia what she wanted and be truthful. "Because he's a total jerk, Cynthia."

She looked up at me without lifting her chin out of her hands. "You think so?"

"Yep, I do. No guy worth his stuff would treat you this way. Not ever. You understand? This isn't about you at all." That part was a tiny lie, but not in the most real sense. In the most real sense, Dillard was an idiot, and an uncaring one at that.

I looked up and saw Daniel standing across the street with Taco, and when he saw me notice him, he walked his fingers to tell me he was going to go up the block and come back. I gave him a small smile of thanks and returned my attention to Cynthia.

Her sobs were slowing now, and I hoped I had been able to help a little. But the truth was, she was possibly a murderer, and I didn't really want to spend a lot of time alone with her, just in case. It didn't seem likely that she could have possibly strangled anyone, not if a break up sent her sobbing to someone she barely knew. But I'd seen stranger behavior in my lifetime.

I stood and gently pulled her up with me before slipping an arm around her shoulder and steering her toward the front door. "This sucks, Cynthia. I'm so sorry."

She let out a hard breath and said, "Yeah, it does." But then she turned to me and said, "But you're okay single, and you're way older than me." She squared her shoulders. "If you're okay, I can be, too."

I chose to ignore the "way older" part and didn't point out that technically I wasn't single-single and cheered her on. "Now there's the spirit," I said and immediately felt like one of those matronly housekeeper types from the British murder mysteries.

At the front door, she turned and said, "Thank you, Harvey."

As soon as she was down the block a bit, Daniel and Taco popped in, and I went to set the alarm and lock the front door. I was ready to go home for the night. It must have been my advanced age, but I was ready for another early bed time.

THE NEXT MORNING, I rushed into the shop early, having remembered my deposit sitting in the safe from the night before. Cynthia's arrival had distracted me, and now that I'd put the money into the proper form and removed it from our cash account books, I didn't want to delay in getting that deposit into the bank.

At nine, as soon as the bank opened, I scooted into the lobby, went to Cynthia's window, gave her a wink, and handed her my deposit bag. She smiled at me warmly, prepared the deposit, and gave me my receipt.

"How are you doing?" I whispered before I left.

"Better. Chubby Hubby Ice Cream always helps," she said with a small smile.

I laughed. "Yes, yes it does." I looked at her closely, and while she still had the sort of forlorn, wary expression of the recently rejected, she did look better, and that made me happy. "You know where to find me if you need a reminder about the jerks of the world."

She laughed. "I'll keep that in mind. Thanks, Harvey."

I walked out of the bank at almost a skip, glad to have the deposit off my mind, relieved that Cynthia seemed much improved, and eager to make good use of this extra bit of time in the store alone. I untied Mayhem from the tree out front and was admiring the window boxes on our faux window mural as I walked up to the shop. Then, I walked right into the chest of a man approaching, dropping everything in my hands.

"I'm so sorry," I said as I bent to pick up my things, and when I looked up, I saw it was Deputy Dillard standing over me. I had the impulse to accidentally knee him somewhere sensitive as I stood, but I restrained myself. "Ah, deputy. I didn't see you there."

He bent to help me pick up my purse and gave Mayhem's ears a good scratch before standing again. "You seem chipper," he said.

I sighed. Neighborliness sometimes was required even when one wasn't feeling neighborly. "I guess I am. Thanks. And you?"

He shrugged. "Pretty good, actually."

I wanted to knee him again, but decided, instead, to smile. "Have a good day then." I moved toward the store, hoping to avoid further conversation, but he caught me.

"Harvey, I just wanted to say that I thought you did a great job with the Henri Johnson ploy. You really had the town believing she was guilty."

I turned back toward him. "That's kind of you to say, but I did realize through that whole rigamarole that lying is not my forte."

He smiled. "Mine neither. It's a good quality, I think."

I forced another smile onto my face. "Well, I'm off to work. Have a good day, Deputy."

"Please call me Chad."

"Have a good day, Chad." I never had liked the name Chad very much.

. . .

Flower sales were swift again that day, and Elle came by mid-morning to say that she was glad we hadn't gone on another few days or she would have been hard-pressed to get us the stems we needed. "As it is now, you have bought all my usual surplus, so I'm going to put in extra tomatoes this year. Use the money to buy some organic starts. Boost my produce sales a bit."

"You know, you could just use the extra money and take a vacation or buy yourself a great pair of shoes or something."

She doubled over with laughter. "Farmers don't get vacations, Harvey. And these," she held up one foot adorned in a bright blue pair of mud-caked boots, "these are the only shoes I need.

I looked down at my well-worn Birkenstock clogs that I swapped out with Birkenstock sandals in the summer and smiled. "These are the booksellers' version."

Elle smiled. "Ah, I thought it was Danskos."

I grinned. "That's the pure East Coast version. I have just enough West Coast in me to go Birk."

I looked over at the buckets of sweet peas and tulips that she'd brought in. All that water made them really heavy. "As long as there's arch support," I said. "Farmers and booksellers both need that."

"Hear! Hear!" Elle said. "I'll be back in a bit. I'm on delivery duty today."

I waved as she headed out and passed Marcus on the way. He dropped his backpack by the register and held up a massive book. "Ah, you finished it," I said with a smile.

"Stayed up half the night. You could have warned me."

"And why would I do that?" I winked as I picked up his copy of *The Goldfinch* and thumbed the pages. "What hooked you?"

We launched into a discussion of Tartt's masterful novel and continued talking about it between customer requests and flower sales. As usual, he was swayed more by the language, and I found the characters and structure the most compelling aspects. But in the end, we both agreed it was one of the best books we'd read in a long time.

Mom, Ariel, Elle, and Daniel came in about eleven-thirty, attached the notes to the flower stems, and headed out for deliveries. Daniel was a brave man and leashed up Mayhem and Taco for the walk, which I appreciated because Mom and Dad had brought their dog, Sidecar, who I thought needed a little special attention. Well, actually, I just wanted some snuggle time with that cute guy, and Mayhem, while willing to share me a little, was not too keen on me getting too friendly with any other dog, Taco excepted. She knew that long, low pooch had his own person, so she didn't get jealous. Sidecar, however, was another story.

The weather was perfect – seventy-two and sunny, and I wanted a little fresh air. So the fuzzy pup and I headed out the back door of the shop for a quick stroll up the alley. I was eager to ponder a plan I had to put some landscaping in back here, if the other shop owners agreed, to make it a little more picturesque and maybe even make some employee parking spaces.

Sidecar and I were strolling along, me envisioning and him peeing, when movement just ahead caught my eye. Our dumpsters were all back here – something I'd have to consider in my landscape plan – so at first, I thought I'd just caught sight of someone tossing a trash bag. But then I looked more closely and saw that two people were walking away from us along the tree line that ran the length of the alley.

I hurried Sidecar along as I squinted to see who was there and gasped. I didn't want to risk them seeing me hurrying back along the alley if they turned around, so I took out my phone and pretended to have a loud, laughing conversation while I walked. I put the phone to my right ear so that my head naturally turned back toward the Main Street buildings and kept walking. Sidecar was no dummy and followed my lead, tugging me on ahead and slightly to the left as we passed Dillard and Cynthia walking with hands entwined.

9

$\mathcal{I}$ kept up my fake phone call for another block, until the alley ended, and then turned the corner back to Main Street before dialing the sheriff's cell. "I don't know how to tell you this . . ."

He was at the shop in five minutes, and while he was livid, this time he didn't storm out for a confrontation. I knew that part of the reason was because he didn't want to involve me, and since I had been clearly visible to Cynthia and Chad, ugh, I hated that name, as I walked away, they would know immediately who ratted them out. But he also had other reasons.

"Harvey, I'm going to need your help again," he said with obvious reluctance.

"Don't sound so excited, Tuck." I tried to make light of a tense moment, but it didn't work. He just stared at me, his mouth a flat line. "Okay, what do you need me to do?"

"Three things. First, I need you to keep doing what you are doing – tell me if you see Cynthia or Cynthia and Dillard at all."

"Okay, got it. Easy enough. Secondly?"

"I need you to work on Cynthia a little for me, see if she'll open up to you more about what happened with the co-op's accounts."

"You want me to see if she'll admit to stealing the money?" I felt a flush of excitement at the prospect.

The sheriff sighed. "Yes, if you can get her that far. But even if she'll just give you a bit more information about who had access to the accounts, who had reason to steal – that kind of thing."

"Alright. And third?"

"I need you to see if Ariel will help." He frowned even as he asked. "I don't like involving civilians, and I particularly don't like involving civilians I don't know very well."

I chuckled. "Civilians. Now who sounds like a TV cop?"

He gave me a small smile. "You know what I mean. It's like it's once removed to have Ariel involved, but I think I need her." He winced a little when he said it.

"Because she knows things?"

"Right. And she's not compromised by Dillard." He shook his head. "I'm sorry, Harvey. I'm afraid I'm having to ask you to do his job."

I crinkled my nose. "Yeah, I guess he can't really be trusted, huh?"

"No, he can't. But until I figure out exactly what's going on there – poor judgment or something more ugly – I can't let him know I know he's now disobeying a direct order for the third time."

"Understood," I said. I looked out at the street and saw Ariel walk by with her much-smaller armload of flowers. "Here's a question, though. Isn't Ariel still a suspect for the robbery?"

"Technically, yes. But I don't think she did either thing – steal from the co-op or murder Wilma. If she'd been able to steal that kind of money for that long, surely she would have stolen enough to get herself an apartment."

I nodded. That made sense. "Plus, she hasn't been there long enough. She's been there three months, but the co-op is behind on the mortgage four months."

"And she just had too much to risk by killing Wilma. A new manager could have meant all new patterns that would have put her ability to stay in the attic in danger."

I let out a long breath. "I'm with you. I'll see what she might know. It's okay if I tell her you asked me to talk to her?"

He nodded. "If you need to, yes. But try to work by sharing as little information as possible."

"Check." I tilted my head and smiled.

"And don't tell her about Dillard and Cynthia," he added.

"Okay, but I suspect she knows they're dating . . . or whatever they're doing. She and Cynthia are friends."

He squeezed his forehead. "Okay, well, she can't know that I've ordered Dillard to stay away."

"Got it." I put my hand on his shoulder and squeezed. "It'll be okay, Tuck. Go rest. I'll be your informal deputy, and just think, you don't even have to pay me."

He chuckled a little. "That *is* a bonus."

THE FINAL HOURS of the flower sale were a frenzy with dozens of people coming in to buy up stems. Some people even came back for their second purchase, so happy with the way the first gifts had made them feel that they wanted to buy more flowers for more people. It was like a wonderfully scented wave of good will in the store, and I wanted to ride that wave.

Sadly, at five-thirty, just before his dinner rush, Max Davies came in. I tried to duck into the café and hide behind Rocky's counter, but he saw me and came over. "I'm here to buy a dozen flowers, red roses if you have them."

I physically restrained a groan while saying, "We can't allow you to pick the type of flower, Max. Sorry. Sale policy."

Rocky kicked me in the shin as she grinned like she was the cat who ate the canary. I kicked her back.

"Well, then, I hope you will pick your favorite flowers to give yourself." He didn't even have the chagrin to blush or look shy when he said that.

"Marcus will sell you the flowers, Max." Rocky said, as she kicked me again. "Thank you."

Then, Max winked, and I couldn't hold back the groan any longer. Fortunately, Rocky happened to turn on the milk steamer at just that moment, and Max didn't hear. He headed to the register to make his purchase.

"Rocky Chevalier, quit kicking me," I said as I tried to disappear into the bakery case both so that Max couldn't talk to me anymore and so I could eat all the breaded things of comfort I could find.

"He is unbelievable, Harvey. He knows about Daniel, right?" Rocky asked while forming a perfect steamed milk heart in my mug.

"Yes, of course he knows. Even the fire hydrants in this town know everything the minute it happens. He just doesn't care."

She grinned as she watched him hand Marcus his cash and then smile over at me. "I'll say. He is determined."

"Well, I wish he'd determine his way to someone else. Oh, he makes me so mad." I felt heat on the tips of my ears.

"Strong feelings, Harvey. Sounds like he's getting the rise he wants."

"Ugh." I kicked her again before I headed back to the register now that Max was safely gone.

Marcus smiled as I walked over. "Don't even start," I said. "Rocky has teased me enough for the both of you."

"Oh, but Rocky doesn't know that Max slipped an extra forty dollars into the sale if I promised to do my best and get you red roses." His smile reached both of his ears.

I dropped my head back on my shoulders. "Tell me you didn't agree."

"Oh, I agreed. Told him that I'd look at the flowers myself in the morning and pick the best ones for you."

I collapsed onto the stool. "You are no help."

"Customer service, Ms. B., Customer service." He laughed as he headed out to tidy up the floor.

I gazed longingly at the pastry case again.

THAT NIGHT, we had all planned to gather at our house to tally the fundraising results and make plans for distribution of the last day's flowers. Mom had gone to all the merchants and gathered the cash and sales totals, and she and Dad were counting bills and running numbers at my kitchen counter when Daniel and I arrived.

Lu and Tuck were bringing dinner for everyone, and Ariel and Mart had gone to get wine and soda for the evening. Soon, Stephen and Walter arrived with Ollie, who had been, apparently, working on a new piece that he was, sort of humorously, sort of hush hush about. Henri and Bear showed up soon after and sent Pickle's regards. Apparently, he and his wife had date night every Wednesday. "Haven't missed a night in twenty-seven years," Henri said, and I found myself imagining Daniel and me in twenty-seven years. I liked the vision.

Rocky and Marcus came over after closing up the store and café, and Elle wandered in wearing muddy overalls and smelling of tomato vines just as the Masons came with supper. Enchiladas, beans and rice, and fried plaintains. I almost swooned when Cate and Lucas arrived with cupcakes, too. Ariel and Mart returned with a case of wine and another of soda, and the party was complete.

We all made ourselves plates and found seats in the living room while we waited for Mom and Dad to finish tallying. I hoped that the delay meant we had huge figures and not some discrepancy in someone's record keeping. But when I saw Mom's face as she came in, I knew that it was the former.

"Folks," she said with tears in her eyes, "we raised $13,815." The tears slid down her cheeks.

I looked over at Ariel, and she had her hands over her mouth as tears pooled on her lashes. I found myself teary, too, and as I looked around the room, the silence of awe settled in with my tearful glances.

"To an end to homelessness," Walter said as he raised a glass into the air.

"An end to homelessness," everyone said and then we cheered for ourselves.

The food tasted especially good after that, and we all enjoyed seconds and even some thirds. It felt good to celebrate in this quiet way with good friends, no fanfare, no public announce-

138   ACF BOOKENS

ment, just an awareness that we had helped a new friend and could help more people as time went on.

Somehow the feeling of success made us a quieter bunch than usual, and so when our cupcakes had been eaten, everyone began to filter home, much to Sasquatch and Sidecar's dismay. They had been quite content to share the island of pillows with Taco and Mayhem. Aslan, however, was elated to see everyone go so that she could have her chenille throw on her couch cushion back, and she reclaimed her space with a flurry of pitty-pattying as soon as Lucas vacated her seat. *The nerve of some people*, her expression said.

Daniel lingered on a bit with Mart, Ariel, and me, but eventually, he yawned and headed out, too, saying he'd see me at noon for the final day of deliveries.

I poured all of us a second glass of wine as we settled into the couch a little deeper, careful not to disturb Aslan's perfect circle of feline comfort. Then, I decided it was the right time to ask for Ariel's help. I kind of wished I'd been able to give Mart the heads up, but she'd follow my lead. She was good like that.

I didn't really know a delicate way to get into this conversation, so when a natural silence rose up, I filled it. "Ariel, I need to ask your help with something."

"Anything," she said, "you guys have done so much for me."

"And you don't owe us anything," I said quickly. "This isn't about you paying us back or anything. You have no debt. None."

Mart nodded. "That's right. It was our honor to help. We are friends. No obligations among friends."

I smiled at my best friend who was, still, picking up more than her financial share of things in this house. "No, this is more about helping Wilma . . . and, well, helping Sheriff Mason."

"Oh," she said with interest. "How can I do that?"

"Well, I'm wondering if you might be able to tell us a bit about how transactions are tracked at the bank," I said tentatively. I wasn't sure exactly what information would be helpful, but that felt like a good place to start.

Ariel sat up a little straighter. "Oh, is this the sleuthing that Stephen said you are prone to do? Do I get to sleuth, too?" She looked downright excited.

Mart groaned. "Not another one."

"Well, this time I actually have permission," I said with my snootiest accent as I stuck out my tongue at my best friend. "Can you help, Ariel?"

"Oh yeah, I can totally help." She leaned forward. "Every transaction at the bank is tagged with date, time, and employee number. That information is accessible by the managers so that we can clarify any confusion for customers if need be."

"So then, it should be very easy to determine who transferred the money between the co-op's accounts," Mart said. "Why hasn't Sheriff Mason done that already?"

Ariel furrowed her brow. "Yeah, it's pretty routine if he has a warrant. If someone at the bank was transferring funds from an account, then there's a record."

Now, I was totally baffled. If the sheriff could locate this information so easily, why not wrap up that part of the case quickly? I sat back in my chair and sipped my wine. "Okay, so there's a reason that the sheriff hasn't asked for that information then, right?"

Mart shook her head. "I suppose so, but if he could catch the thief, wouldn't that get him a bit closer to solving the murder?"

Ariel's head whipped up. "Wait, so this is about more than the co-op's money?"

I gave Mart a significant stare, and a flush went up her neck. "Oops, were we keeping the possible connection on the down-low?"

I sighed. "That had been the plan." I turned to Ariel. "No offense, Ariel. The sheriff just didn't want to jump to conclusions or spread rumors, you know?"

Ariel was staring off into space and didn't even acknowledge my words. I watched her, and then, she gave her head a little shake. "What were you saying? Oh, right. Yeah, no worries about that. I get it. But here's the thing, what if the theft and the murder are connected, but the sheriff wants most people to think they aren't?"

I pursed my lips. "Tell us more."

"Okay, so if the sheriff gets that transaction information, and if it shows that someone at the bank has been stealing from the co-op, then he has to make an arrest, right?"

Mart and I nodded.

"But what if he doesn't want to make the arrest just yet because he needs the person at the bank to still be there?"

"Or maybe he doesn't want to tip someone off about what he's actually up to?" I added.

"You think he's doing another bait and switch?" Mart asked.

Ariel looked puzzled, and we caught her up on the ruse with Henri and the murder. "Oh, right. Like that. Right. Keep everyone involved clueless since he needs more time to gather evidence on the murder."

I had to admit, the woman was good. I thought maybe she was

right, but what I couldn't figure out now was why Tuck would have me talk to Ariel about the bank if he knew this all along. Unless . . . "Tuck is using me as the bait again," I said almost under my breath.

"Sounds like it," Mart said, "and he knew you couldn't lie to save your life, so he thought it best to not tell you the whole story."

I grumbled quietly but then took a deep breath and realized that he'd been right to not tell me. "Still, he had to know I'd figure out that what he was asking me to research was very fundamental. So why even ask at all?"

Ariel fell back against her seat. "I think I know who is stealing from the co-op."

I sat forward, distracted from my own question by this new information. "You do?"

"Yeah, well, maybe." She shook her head, and I saw her set her jaw. "I think I know, but I don't want to say anything until I'm sure. I can check tomorrow."

I nodded. I appreciated that she respected people's privacy and wanted to be certain, but I was dying to know.

"But I still can't figure out why the sheriff wanted you to talk to me? That just doesn't make sense. If all it takes is a little searching on the computer . . ."

We sat quietly sipping our wine for a bit, and no matter which way I looked at it, I couldn't figure out the sheriff's plan . . . and since I knew he had one and didn't want to flub up any attempt to capture a murderer, I thought I'd better ask.

"I'm texting him now. We need more information," I announced.

"We do. If we're going to be the bait, we need to at least be informed bait," Mart agreed.

"That's right. We aren't earthworms after all," Ariel said with forcefulness.

"Not minnows either," Mart added.

"Not even chunks of hot dog," I chimed in, and the two other women laughed.

"Hot dog?" Mart asked.

"That's what Dad used to make me fish with since I wouldn't put a worm on the hook."

We cracked up from the stress and the silliness and a bit from the wine, too. But the mood got more serious quickly when the sheriff said he'd be right over.

"Oh, this is a big deal. It's close to ten o'clock," I said.

"Whew, soon we'll be up to eleven like young people," Mart snarked with a wink at Ariel.

"Don't look at me. I fell asleep about eight most nights when I was in the bank. There's only so much reading a person can do with a headlamp," Ariel said.

Her quip reminded me of what Dillard had told me. "Ariel, I know we talked about books before, but I have a question about the attic. You had a lot of books up there?

"Yep. I like to have options for when the mood strikes." She looked at me sideways. "Why?"

"She's on to you, Harvey. She knows you never ask an idle question." Mart winked with exaggeration.

"You're right. Dillard mentioned it to me, and I thought it was odd that he would know that. Did he know you were living in the attic?"

Ariel shook her head. "Not that I know of. Cynthia knew, of course, but she'd never been up there with me so she wouldn't have seen the stacks of books I borrowed from the library. She's not much of a reader either. We didn't talk books or anything, so I don't think I would have mentioned it except maybe in passing.

I tilted my head. "Cynthia could have told Dillard, but why would she have mentioned something like that to him?" I was getting that feeling that I was on the cusp of understanding something when I heard a knock at the door and got up to let the sheriff in.

Sheriff Mason looked ragged and worn down, and while he was polite and friendly, he didn't exactly look happy to see us. "Ladies," he said as he sat on the edge of the couch.

"Can I get you something to drink, Tuck?"

"Hot tea?" He smiled.

"You got it," Mart said as she headed to our electric kettle on the counter.

"You needed to ask me something, Harvey?"

I sighed. "I did. We all did. And I hope the question isn't rude, but why did you ask me to find out about the banking stuff when you could easily figure that out?"

This time, Tuck sighed, and when he met my eyes, they sparked. "Because I knew you could get to the bottom of the question without me, Harvey, and I needed to not be involved with finding out that information."

I narrowed my eyes. "Because you need to keep someone thinking that you're still thinking of the two investigations as separate?

He nodded. "Right. I think I may know what is happening at the bank, and I'm pretty sure I know who killed Wilma. But I need more information about both—"

"But you didn't want to tip anyone off about how much you did know, so Harvey's, um, curiosity became an asset," Mart said as she came back with a cup of chamomile tea and handed it to the sheriff.

Tuck put a finger on his nose. "You got it, Mart. I knew you'd wonder about my motives sooner rather than later, Harvey, especially when you figured out how easy it would be track transactions. Still, I was hoping to buy some time."

Ariel cleared her throat. "So yeah, it is easy to track transactions, but it's also kind of easy – especially in a small bank like ours, where transactions aren't checked by committee like they are at bigger banks – to use someone else's credentials to do a transaction."

"Like a name and password kind of thing?" Mart asked.

"Just like that. If someone knew someone else's name and password . . ."

"They could steal from the co-op *and* frame someone else for the theft," I said softly. "I'm sure you thought of that already, too, right?" I looked at the sheriff, but he was staring off into space. "Sheriff?"

He gave his head a little shake and looked back at me. "Sorry, just putting it all together." He set his mug down on the coffee table with a hard thud.

Ariel leaned forward. "Sheriff, I can get the information on the transactions tomorrow morning if that would help." She looked at him hopefully. "I can be discreet, and I'd really like to help."

The sheriff frowned. "I know that I asked Harvey to talk to you, but just to confirm what I suspected about how the systems worked. I'm not sure I'm comfortable with you actually gathering information. Besides, none of it would be admissible in court."

Ariel nodded. "But would it be helpful to just know? Then you could gather more evidence and get your warrant when the time was right?"

The sheriff sat back against the couch, and I picked up his mug and put it in his hand. "What if I went into the bank on the premise of looking at a loan for the store and was there with Ariel when she accessed the information? That way, I can carry the information out, and she doesn't even have to make a phone call or anything."

Mart grimaced at me, but she didn't say anything.

Ariel chuckled. "It's not like looking up the information is going to look that much different than what I normally do, but if you'd like to be there, Harvey, by all means."

I felt my face flush. Busted. My nosiness wasn't so subtle.

"Actually, I like that idea, only because I'd like two pairs of eyes on the information since we won't be getting print outs or anything at this point."

"Ha!" I shouted. "See!" I looked at Mart and winked. She just rolled her eyes.

THE NEXT MORNING, before I went in for my normal eleven a.m. start, I stopped by the bank. I made sure I came with a notebook and my laptop just so I looked official. During breakfast, I even worked up what I might do with a loan if I actually applied for one. It had been fun to figure out what I could use more money for, and I landed on more shelving that would take my shelves to the ceiling, allowing me to store my extra stock on the floor, and then convert the back room to a staff lounge and reading group space down the road. In fact, by the time I was done imagining, I had decided to ask Ariel to actually run the numbers for me. I knew I couldn't afford to take on a loan this early in our business, and I still needed to get my own salary up so that I could give more to our household expenses. But I wanted some real figures to work with down the road.

I went through the standard process, which Ariel had explained the night before, and approached the teller counters to ask if I could speak to someone about a business loan. Cynthia was there, and when I walked up to her window, she gave me a wide smile. "Hi Harvey. It's good to see you. What can I do for you?"

I tried to act natural and said, "I'm just here to talk to Ariel about a loan. Is she available?"

Cynthia frowned. "Right." She looked at me askance for a minute and then said, "I'll let her know you're here."

I wasn't sure why Cynthia seemed, well, annoyed, but I figured paying too much attention to that might give me away. I ignored the hesitation in her voice and gave a hearty thanks.

Fortunately, Ariel was available, and Cynthia pointed me to her office at the back of the lobby. I could feel her watching me as I walked that way.

Everyone in town knew Ariel was living at my house temporarily, so we didn't need to pretend to meet. But still, we did need our bit of theater to be believable. We'd worked out the night before that we'd say we talked about the loan casually but that Ariel had asked me to come in so she could put together a formal proposal for me. She didn't know that I'd actually decided to consider the proposal, but I figured that fact would just make things all the more believable.

Once I was in Ariel's office, we had a bit of privacy, but the offices didn't have doors, so we still had to be discreet about our query. I made a point of explaining to Ariel what I was considering for the shop and telling her how much I thought it would cost to have Woody increase our shelving in the store. Then, she gave me information on interest rates and the application process. Finally, she said, "If you'll look here, you can see the various options for payment plans and how that works out in terms of interest." She spun her computer so that it faced the wall of her office, making it so that I could see the screen but no one out in the lobby could.

There, I saw a series of transactions, all for the exact amount of Cate's mortgage payments and each was going into the account of one Renee Forsham. I contained my gasp when I saw the name of Wilma's sister. Whoa!!

Ariel must have noticed my shock because she said, "Oh yes, that five-year repayment plan does pack a punch in terms of the size of the payments."

"It does. I was caught off guard." I gave her a small smile.

"Let me rework those numbers a bit, see if we can't give you terms that work better for your budget." She turned the computer back toward herself and typed for a few moments. "Okay, how does this look?"

She turned the computer back toward me, and I peered at the screen. "Oh, well, yes, that's more what I was expecting." There on the screen was Cynthia's name and what I assumed was her employee ID number. I hadn't memorized the transaction information from the previous screen, but the number of transactions matched.

"Me, too." Ariel looked stricken. Her friend had been the one stealing. Oh, that had to hurt.

I leaned back in the wooden chair in front of Ariel's desk and tried to think of some coded way to offer my sympathy. "Even expecting it, though, it's hard information to take in. I'll have to think about it. Is that okay?"

Ariel took a deep breath and pulled herself back to her professional guise. "Of course. Just let me know if you decide you want to move forward." She stood up and shook my hand, but then I grabbed her in a quick hug, counting on the fact that we were friends to explain this unusual behavior between a loan officer and a potential borrower.

She squeezed me hard and whispered. "I'll come by a bit later. We can talk then."

I walked out with a printout of my actual loan offer in my hand. I gave Cynthia a small wave and smile as I walked through the lobby. But as soon as I got out the door, my smile dropped. What exactly did Renee Forsham have to do with all of this?

I texted Mart with an update as I walked quickly over to the store. She sent back her Memoji with a blown mind, and I chuckled as I swung open the door to the shop and walked right into Renee Forsham.

Then, I dropped my phone and almost fell over picking it up. Luckily, my clumsiness bought me a second to pull myself together.

"Oh, hi, Renee. Sorry, shouldn't text and walk."

She gave me a forced smile. "Probably wise." She smoothed off the front of her suit and sighed.

"You're mighty dressed up for a town where even the fancy French restaurant throws out newspaper for a crab boil once a month." I smiled with an expression that I hoped seemed casual and warm.

"I was at my sister's attorney's office this morning. Finalizing her estate."

I nodded. "I see. I'm sorry. I expect that was hard."

She looked at me with a blank expression for just a second before forcing her face into a sorrowful pout. "Yes, very. I mean, I wouldn't take any money in the world if I could have my sister back."

I nodded and tried to look sympathetic while also trying not to fidget with my phone and text Tuck immediately. "It's nice she thought of you, though. I take it she left you something?" I was trying to be casual, and for a second, I thought Renee was on to me because a grimace flashed over her face.

"It is nice to be thought of, of course." The flatness of her voice made me think it was anything but nice. "Mostly, I miss her, you know?"

"I can imagine." I stepped around her gently and let her follow me into the store. "Did you need something from me?"

She looked puzzled.

"You were in the shop. I didn't know if you were buying books or needed me in particular." I was pretty eager to get away from this thief, but I figured this might be my only chance to get some information.

"Oh, right. Right. Yes, I came to let you know that the memorial service will be on Saturday. We're doing it at ten a.m. at the Baptist church up the road."

"Thank you for letting me know. Is it for family only or might a few of us who knew Wilma also come?"

"Please come. Wilma would have loved to have you there."

I kept my face blank, but the idea of Wilma Painter wanting anyone in her vicinity was laughable. I wondered if Renee really believed that or if she was just putting up a front to act the grieving sister.

"I'll be there, then. Thank you for letting me know."

Renee nodded once and then turned and walked back out the door.

There was no way I could get all this into a text, so I checked in with Marcus and then headed out to meet Tuck, who had suggested tacos at Lu's truck since it was nearly lunch time. I never passed up a chance to have one of Lu's tacos.

When I arrived, Lu had propped open the back door of the truck, and Tuck was sitting there with a plate on his lap and one beside him. "Two carnitas, right?" he said as he lifted the plate from the metal step.

"You know me too well, Lu," I said into the truck's interior. All I heard was a laugh in return.

"You will not believe what we found out," I said before promptly taking a huge bite of taco. The sheriff waited patiently while I chewed and I got more and more embarrassed at my own rudeness. Then I filled him in on what Ariel and I found out about Cynthia and Renee Forsham. Then I told him about Renee's visit to the lawyer and the memorial service.

He quietly ate his tacos and listened, but he didn't look surprised at all.

"You knew all this?"

"I suspected. Not the part about Renee. That's new. But Cynthia, I thought it was probably her."

"Yeah, Ariel, too. Poor thing. They are friends." I shook my head.

"Always hard when people disappoint you." He wiped his

mouth with a napkin from his knee. "Still, better to know now before you find yourself in the midst of something you don't want to be a part of."

"True. Still, why do you think Cynthia did it?"

"Greed probably. That's usually the reason for theft," Tuck said matter-of-factly.

"And Renee? The same reason?"

"Probably. I'll have to check with that lawyer about the estate. That should be easy, a routine part of the investigation."

I took another bite of my taco and leaned back against the frame of the food truck's door. "Surely Renee wouldn't have stolen if she'd thought she was going to come into sizable money when her sister died."

"Well, she didn't know her sister would die anytime soon." Tuck raised an eyebrow. "It doesn't sound like she came into sizable money, though."

"Yeah, she was clearly displeased." I took another bite of taco and watched people walk by on the street for a while. "Any closer to arresting anyone?"

"Maybe," he said with a shrug and a grin.

I groaned and smiled. "Thanks for the tacos, you information miser." I shoved the last half of my second one in my mouth as I stood up.

Tuck laughed. "Thanks for the info, Harvey." He stepped up into the truck and kissed Lu on the cheek before climbing down and joining me as we walked back toward Main Street, Mayhem tugging me all the way.

"You'll keep me posted?" I asked hopefully.

"Anything you need to know, my dear, you'll know," the sheriff said with a laugh as he headed toward the station.

ONE OF THE things that I liked best about Marcus was that he was always paying attention but didn't feel the need to know everything, unlike me. When I came back in the shop, he waved from where he was helping a customer in the history section, but after he rang up the customer's copy of *Master of the Mountain*, he just asked how I was. No prying. No nudging for more information when clearly there was some to give.

I wished I could be more like him. For a minute. Then I started to ponder how I could figure out what Renee Forsham's involvement was in all this.

I didn't get far, though, because we had a very full day of flower deliveries to contend with, and it was all hands on deck for attaching notes. Mom and Dad, Henri and Bear, Ariel, Daniel, Cate and Lucas, Mart, Elle, Rocky, and even Woody with his sausage-size fingers spread out over the café while Marcus staffed the store. I stood at the café counter and directed flower and note dispersal, tucking my own flowers from Max under the counter so that I could avoid the inevitable teasing. The man was ridiculous, and I didn't feel like dealing with him or my friends and their snide commentary.

Our chatter was minimal since we were already behind schedule on getting these out the door. We simply hadn't anticipated how many flowers would get ordered on this last day, and we were rushing to get everything delivered on time.

The practice we'd come to was to group flowers in a single bucket if they were going to a similar location – this end of Main Street versus that end, the school, the hospital, etc. Today, I noticed that a lot of flowers were accumulating in one bucket, and Elle quickly got a second for that location. As we attached notes, those buckets became full and Elle brought over a third. Curious as always, I stopped my work and took a look at the scrap of paper with the label – North Main Street. So here, near the store.

I then looked at the list of notes I had to attach and saw that most of mine were going to Cynthia at the bank. Sheriff Mason might believe in coincidences, but this seemed too much. The same was true for most of the flowers – some four dozen – in the buckets Elle had put aside. When we were done addressing, I counted. Cynthia had five dozen flowers coming to her.

We hadn't recorded names of the people sending the flowers or notes, but from the tenor of the messages, it was clear this person was quite the admirer. "I can't wait to see you tonight." "Remember that afternoon in the park? Your lips." We had required that all messages be PG-rated, or I had a feeling this flower giver might have been more amorous in their affections.

I decided to deliver Cynthia's flowers myself, play off my visit to Ariel a bit. I didn't think anyone could have known what we were doing, but then, I was not always the best actress, as we'd discovered.

I couldn't manage any more deliveries with sixty flowers in my arms, so Daniel came along with the rest of the stems for this part of town. We walked quickly to the bank, and as I came through the door with the massive armload of flowers, the employees gasped with delight. The mood cooled considerably, though, as I walked to Cynthia's window and handed her all the flowers.

Her eyes got wide, and she said, "All of these are for me?"

I nodded. "You seem to have quite the admirer." I winked and smiled, even though I was not feeling very charitable toward her at this moment. You cross my friends, you cross me, and Cynthia had definitely crossed Cate.

She read a few of the notes, and the blush ran up her cheeks.

"Sounds like the good officer has come around?"

Her eyes flew to my face, and she looked shocked. "Why would you say that?"

Now, it was my turn to be puzzled. "Because just a few days ago you were quite upset about—" I stopped talking because Cynthia looked like she was going to pass out. I took a hold of her arm, straining to reach over the high counter between us. "Are you okay?"

"I can't believe this. I can't believe she would do this." Cynthia shook her head. "I can't believe it."

I resisted asking more questions and, instead, gestured to Daniel for help. He had been waiting by the door but must have been watching because he was already on his way with the bank manager.

"Cynthia here has had a shock," I said to the manager. "Would it be alright if we took her outside for some fresh air?"

The young woman nodded, clearly uncomfortable with the situation, and as we helped Cynthia to the front door, I saw another teller gather her flowers and head toward the back of the bank. I hoped she was going to put them in water.

Outside, we steered Cynthia to a bench and suggested she put her head between her knees, which she did without a word.

A few minutes later, the color came back to her face, and she sat up with a deep sigh. "Thank you. I was just so shocked." She winced out a smile. "Just so many flowers."

I patted her back. "Of course, you know who they were from?" I tried to sound playful.

Some of the color left her face again. "From Chad, of course."

I pursed my lips. "Oh, I thought you said 'she' in there."

Cynthia gave a rough laugh. "You must have misheard me. They have to be from Chad. Who else could they be from?"

That was exactly the question I was asking, but I decided now was not the time to push the point. "You okay?"

"I am. Thanks." She stood up and squared her shoulders. "Thanks for bringing the flowers." She turned and went back inside.

Daniel picked up his bucket, and I untied Taco and Mayhem from the tree outside, and we continued up the street to deliver our remaining few flowers.

Before we stepped into the yarn shop at the end of the block, Daniel gave me a sideways grin and said, "She, huh?"

"Indeed." I wiggled my eyebrows. "And this mystery is totally mine to solve."

10

*A*s soon as we got back to the shop, I pulled out the list of flower purchases that Mom had collected from the various merchants the previous day. Right there, clear as anything, was the purchase of five dozen stems for three hundred dollars. Paid for in cash at Chez Cuisine.

Daniel read over my shoulder and started to snicker as soon as he saw that the flowers had been bought at Max's restaurant. "Someone is going to be so excited to see you, Ms. Mystery Solver."

"You could at least feign jealousy," I said with a pout.

Daniel forced his grin into a scowl. "Do I have reason to be jealous?"

I smacked him on the arm and told him we were eating out that night. "If I have to bear up under that man's affection, you're going with me."

"Oh, I think I have plans—"

"Daniel Galena, you are coming to dinner with me tonight or else."

That brought out a big smile on his face, and he bent to kiss my cheek. "I'll be here at seven, and I'm leaving Taco to watch after my interests."

I smiled and looked over at the two dogs sound asleep next to the register. "You probably need a better partner for that work. I don't think that guy is watching anything."

AS THE AFTERNOON PASSED, I helped a few customers and drank a couple of cups of decaf, even though I really wanted the fully leaded stuff. I felt like I might need it to get through dinner.

About four, Mom and Dad came back in, and I could tell they were bursting with news. They were practically bouncing as they approached the register.

"Don't tell me. You got another dog?" I said with a wink at Sidecar.

"Even better," Mom said at the same moment that Dad said, "Don't give your mother any ideas."

Mom glared at him and then turned back to me. "Do you want to know or do you just want to keep making wisecracks?"

"Well, if you're going to get mean about it—"

"Ariel's apartment is ready. We can sign the lease, and she can move in tomorrow, if she wants to."

I did a little awkward happy dance behind the register. "That is great news. I'm texting her right now."

Mom grinned. "Copy me in. I want to see what she says."

"Ariel, you up for a move tomorrow?"

Her almost instantaneous reply, "Will I sound rude if I say, YAAAASSSS!"

I sent her a bunch of smiling emojis and told her we'd get her moved tomorrow afternoon. I hoped our friends would be willing to help.

She replied with, "And then we'll have a pizza party at my new place."

"Great plan."

Mom chimed in then. "I'm bringing salad." Mom still hadn't quite gotten the hang of tone in texts yet.

"Salad is great. Mama B," Ariel responded, and I thought my mother might just melt into a puddle of delight right there. Mama B.

I sent my standard three heart reply and put my phone down. "Mom, in addition to salad, can you arrange for the pizzas and maybe see if you can round up folks to help with the move? I have dinner plans tonight that I can't miss—"

"Consider it done. Your dad and I have already located some used furniture for her – a couch, a couple of chairs, a bed frame, and I expect everyone else will have things to contribute," Mom said without letting me finish. "You worry about figuring out the story of the flowers. I'll furnish the apartment and throw a housewarming party."

"How did you know about . . . never mind. Just remember, this is a small apartment, and a casual party. No ice sculptures."

Mom snapped her fingers. "Darn, I was hoping for an ice swan." She winked as she headed out the door with my dad close behind her. He gave me a wave as the bell over the door dinged.

I hadn't been sure I was going to like having my parents live this close, but it was turning out to be a very comforting, not to mention helpful situation. I think they were liking it, too. I had gotten my thrill of helpfulness straight from my mom, so she was in her element at the moment.

Marcus's shift ended at four, but he always stayed over for a bit, mostly in the café. I smiled to myself when I saw him leaning on the counter talking to Rocky. They looked so comfortable with each other, and it made my ever-romantic heart happy.

As he left, he said, "Have fun at dinner," and I swear he made kissing sounds as the door closed behind him. Clearly, everyone thought Max's crush was quite the joke. I didn't take it seriously, but it sure was embarrassing, not to mention just the slightest bit discomforting. I mean, he knew Daniel and I were together, but that didn't slow him down at all. Dinner was going to be all kinds of awkward.

STILL, when Daniel showed up at seven with a collared shirt and smelling of his unique blend of aftershave and motor oil, I couldn't help but be a little excited about our date, even if it involved endless flirtation from a man I had no interest in and endless teasing about said flirtation from the man I loved.

I closed up the shop and found myself grateful that I'd at least taken the time to put some pomade in my hair that morning so that my curls looked intentional instead of their usual blender-inspired style. We walked the half-block to the restaurant, and I made a point of enjoying those few moments in the mild air of spring.

The evening was so lovely that we hoped to dine at the outdoor tables and keep Mayhem and Taco with us, and, fortunately, there was one table for two left on the sidewalk when we arrived. I needed to talk with Max, but I was optimistic that this seating arrangement would postpone my interaction with him until just before we left.

My optimism was not warranted, and I made a note to give the hostess who must have tipped Max off the evil eye next time I saw her. I expected she'd been instructed to tell him any time I came by, but she could have at least let me get one glass of wine down before letting him know. Instead, he came bustling out with a bottle of red wine, already opened, and proceeded to tell us – well, me, really – all about its vintage before pouring a taste into my glass.

I stared at him and then at the wine and then back at him. "I don't drink red wine. Sulfites. They give me migraines."

The look on his face was one of horror, and at first, I thought it was because he realized his faux pas in assuming, well, assuming about a billion things about me and Daniel. But when he scoffed and said, "Nonsense. You have just not had the right red wine. The stuff in the boxes does not even count as wine," I realized that my mistake was thinking that Max could ever admit he was imperfect.

"I assure you, Max. I have had very good red wine in my day, and I simply can't drink it. The pain is not worth it, even for the best of the best."

"I love red wine, though, if you want to leave the bottle," Daniel said, trying to salvage the bottle of wine, if not the moment.

Max acted as if he had not even heard Daniel speak and stormed off, bottle in hand, shouting to the hostess about finding a bottle of chardonnay for our table. I love chardonnay, so I didn't protest.

Our dinner was delicious as it always was at Chez Cuisine. I had the mushroom risotto for about the fifteenth time, and Daniel got fish. We chatted about work and about the flower sale. Daniel assured me that he'd take the next afternoon off to help Ariel move, and I told him about Mom's plan for a housewarming party.

"Do I need to rent a tux?" he asked with a smirk.

"I'll check." I said just as Max returned, this time with a single plate holding what looked to be a tower of chocolate.

"You will not have red wine, so you cannot enjoy the full depth of flavor in the chocolate here, but still, you deserve something delicious and decadent." He set the plate before me and stood waiting by the table.

I looked from him to the cake and then over to Daniel before grabbing a spoonful of the chocolate and passing the cake to Daniel so he could get his share. I loved this man for many reasons, but his quick wit was one of the main ones. "Max, it is incredibly kind of you to get us this romantic dessert to share. Thank you."

I felt fairly certain Max's blood pressure had just skyrocketed, but I needed him not to have a heart attack right there. So I put on my most sweet voice and said, "Really, Max. Thank you. I appreciate the cake. It's delicious."

You might have thought I pledged my undying affection given his reaction. He grabbed my hand and kissed it, his lips staying – as usual – far too long on my skin. "I knew you'd like it. Perhaps someday you will allow me to give you a private lesson on how to make it." He leered at me, and I tried not to shiver.

"That's a kind offer," I said, doing my best to equivocate. "Actually, there is something you can help me with."

"Anything," he said with such innuendo that I felt myself backing up in my chair.

"Someone came in here on Wednesday and bought five dozen flowers for a young woman at the bank. Do you remember who that was?"

He nodded. "Oh yes, Renee. Renee Forsham. Said something about wanting to thank one of her sister's employees."

I stared at Max, trying to process what he'd just told me and realized too late that my gaze was being taken as an invitation.

"Harvey, if I may," he turned his body so that his back was to Daniel, "I would be honored if I could take you to dinner tomorrow night in Annapolis. I know this charming seafood place – small, intimate." He leaned over me as he continued to speak. "We would have a marvelous evening—"

"I have plans tomorrow, Max, and I don't eat seafood. Thank you, though."

Daniel kicked me under the table, and I realized that I was opening myself up to continued advances if I didn't just say no, so I did. "And Max, I am completely dedicated to Daniel." I pointed across the table at my boyfriend who was, to his credit, looking either on the verge of giving Max a few choice words or breaking into hysterical laughter. "I will not go out with you now or ever. Please stop asking."

I must have been speaking loudly because people at several nearby tables turned to look at us. Max, however, was not chagrined in the slightest. "Harvey, dear, you have not yet dissuaded me from my pursuit. Perseverance is always reward-ed." Then he bowed to me slightly and walked back inside.

The waiter brought our check, and we paid promptly and then skittered down the street, trying to contain our laughter until we were out of earshot. When we got to the corner where we left Main Street to head to my house, Daniel couldn't contain himself any longer and turned to me, bowing, and said, "My lady, I am your valiant knight. I will fight to the death for your honor, even if you would rather I not. That is the kind of knight I am."

I rolled my eyes. "I don't know what else to do, Daniel. I've told him no again and again, and he just doesn't listen."

He pulled me close. "I don't know what the answer is, but as long as you're saying no, I'm good." Then he held me at arm's length for a second. "I mean, I'm good if you are. If you want me to speak to him, I will."

I smiled. "Thank you. You are my knight in shining armor, but for now Lady Harvey has it handled. Be on standby, though, lest I need you to joust for me."

We walked a bit further in companionable silence, but then I said, "Renee Forsham is sending amorous notes to Cynthia. Do you think they were seeing each other?"

I saw Daniel's brow crinkle, a sign he was thinking. "I don't know. I don't think so. The way Cynthia reacted . . . she wasn't embarrassed. It was more like she was scared."

He was right. Cynthia had looked terrified. At the time, I thought it was because she knew Dillard wasn't supposed to be seeing her, but now, with this new information, I could see that she had actually been very, very afraid. "Poor girl."

Daniel looked across his shoulder at me. "Harvey, the woman stole from your friend, one of your best friends."

"I know. I know. I'm not saying she's not culpable, but something is going on here, something that makes me think Cynthia may be a victim in this, too."

THE NEXT MORNING, almost as soon as Marcus came in at eleven, I headed to the bank with our deposit. I'd held it again so that I could take it over in person as an excuse to talk to Cynthia.

As soon as I walked in the lobby, I saw her behind the counter, waiting on a customer. I stood in line, letting tellers take other customers until Cynthia was free. When she saw me, she grimaced but then tried to turn it into a smile.

I walked up and handed her my deposit envelope, and then I quietly said, "Cynthia, you don't have to tell me anything, but if you're in some kind of trouble, I'd like to help."

Cynthia kept counting my money and preparing my deposit. Then, she wrote something on a slip of paper and handed it back to me with my receipt and envelope. It felt a bit like a reverse bank robbery. "Have a good day, Ms. Beckett," she said with a stiff smile.

"Thank you, Cynthia. You, too." I held off on opening the note until I got outside, but then I flipped the piece of paper over and read. "I'll come to the store on my lunch break."

Bingo. I knew it. She was in trouble, and I was going to get to help. I realized that there was something wrong with reveling in another person's misery because it made me feel useful, but that was a psychological problem to tackle another day. I hurried back to the store so that I would be there whenever Cynthia came by.

But as I waited, Mart's voice started sounding in my head. "Harvey, don't be too trusting. She could be playing you." I tried to shake off that doubt, but I knew that my imaginary Mart was right. Cynthia was in something deep, and she knew I knew. Maybe she was going to try to scam me . . . or worse. I had to have my guard up.

I was grateful she was coming to the store since it was a public place and the weekend tourist traffic had started to come in. There wasn't much opportunity for me to be in danger. Still, I was glad Marcus was there. I gave him a heads up that Cynthia was coming by and that I wasn't sure what she might tell me. "Can you keep an eye on us?"

"You got it, Ms. B." He nodded solemnly but then a little smile crossed his lips. "How was dinner at Chez Cuisine last night?"

I groaned. "Don't ask."

CYNTHIA CAME in just after noon, and I pointed to the chairs in the fiction section. She shook her head. "I need to look like I'm shopping."

"Oh, right. Okay. Romances?"

"Perfect." We strolled over to the romance shelves and feigned interest in the newest Megan Squires titles.

"So what's going on, Cynthia? The flowers?"

She shot me a look and then stared at the shelf in front of her. "I guess you know Dillard didn't send them."

"I do." I didn't feel like I needed to lie to her about that.

"She's blackmailing me." Cynthia's voice was so quiet that I almost didn't hear her.

"What?! How?" I wasn't quite ready to let her know that I knew about the theft from the co-op accounts.

Cynthia sighed. "About a year ago, Wilma caught me stealing from a customer's safety deposit box that they had neglected to lock. It was a few hundred dollars, something I justified by saying it was my hazard pay for working for Wilma."

"Oh," I said. "What did Wilma do?"

"She actually was very kind. She made me tell the customer, pay back all the money with interest, and let them decide if they wanted to press charges. They didn't. I think because Wilma went to bat for me. But she didn't fire me, and she didn't turn me in herself." Cynthia let out a long, slow breath. "It was the kindest thing anyone had ever done for me."

I wanted to ask why Cynthia had been stealing, but I knew that wasn't the point, so I let it go. "Okay, that does sound kind. But how does Renee fit in?"

"Well, Wilma told her sister about the incident, I guess, and the next thing I knew Renee was opening accounts at our branch and then threatening me if I didn't transfer money into them. She wanted fifteen hundred a month at least or she'd go to the police."

I put my hands up over my head and looked up at the ceiling. "So you took the easy money in the co-op accounts?" I was grateful that I didn't have to tell Cynthia that Ariel had already figured that out for us.

"I'm so sorry, Harvey. So sorry. I just didn't know what else to do. I didn't want to go to prison."

I nodded. "I get it. I mean, I don't like it, but I get it." I picked up another book and pretended to show it to Cynthia. "But why did Renee want the money? Was she broke?"

"I don't know. It felt personal." She shook her head. "A couple times she said things like, 'Wait until the FDIC gets wind of this.' Like she really just wanted Ms. Painter to get in trouble."

"Ah, so this was some sort of sibling thing," I asked.

"Yeah, but maybe more than that, too. I'm not sure. She seemed kind of scared, too, worried. But I don't know why."

My brain was working fast, but I didn't have enough information to put it all together. "And the flowers?"

"She's kind of into me, I think. I'm not sure. She keeps asking me to dinner, and I keep finding excuses, hoping that she won't get mad and turn me in. But those flowers, they were really creepy."

She stared at her hands. "We never did anything, Ms. Beckett. I don't know what she was talking about – the park, and my mouth and all that."

"Oh man, yeah, that is creepy. Maybe she was setting you up or something?" I kind of hoped that's what it was. Otherwise, Renee Forsham sounded like a stalker.

"Cynthia, I think you need to tell the sheriff what you've told me." I said this gently, hoping not to cause her to panic.

But she surprised me and said, "Yeah, I know. That's why I came here. Ariel told me about how you helped her tell him about where she was living." She looked at me with round eyes. "Will you go with me?"

I honestly didn't really feel like being another escort for a girl with a confession, but I also didn't know how to say no. Cynthia was obviously in distress, and it was equally obvious that Renee Forsham was not the kind, grieving sister she'd made herself out to be. I agreed to go, as support, but also out of curiosity.

As we walked to the station, I texted the sheriff and told him Cynthia and I were coming over "with another confession."

"Oh, okay. See you soon," was his reply. I was again impressed by his ability to be nonplussed no matter what.

At the station, Tuck greeted us at the front desk and walked us back to his office. I knew he was probably expecting some of our conversation, and I appreciated that he used discretion but also didn't make this feel like a casual visit.

As soon as we sat down, Cynthia started talking, and she didn't stop until she'd told the sheriff everything from the theft to the blackmail to the dozens of flowers.

Tuck listened and made notes, asked questions for clarification, and reassured Cynthia, as I had done on the walk over, that once

Cate understood the situation, she would not want to press charges.

To that effect, I took the liberty of discreetly texting Cate the most crucial info to which she replied, "Oh, how awful! How is Cynthia?"

I knew she'd get it. "Okay, but shaken up, of course."

"Of course. I need to get our money back, but please tell her that I'm sorry she was put through that."

"I will."

By the time Cynthia had told Tuck everything, she looked both relieved and exhausted, and Tuck offered to have Harriet, the dispatcher, drive her home. "Thank you, but I need to go back to work."

"Actually," Tuck said, "I want you to stay away from the bank today. I'll talk to your manager. Let her know what's going on. You need to be away from any interaction with Renee Forsham, okay?"

Cynthia's eyes got very wide. "I'm not in any danger, am I?"

The sheriff came around the desk and sat down in front of her. "No, I don't think so. But just to be safe, can you stay with a friend tonight?"

Before Cynthia could say something silly about Dillard or such, I spoke up. "We're having Ariel's housewarming party tonight after we move her in. Why don't you hang with me at the shop until we close? Then you can help us move her in and stay the night with Mart and me. Sound okay?"

Our guest room was getting a lot of use. I made a mental note to text Mart and give her the 411.

Cynthia let out a shuddering sigh. "Okay. If it's not too much trouble."

"No trouble at all. I think Mart might even have some clothes you can borrow." I stood up and stretched. "I'm a bit, um, wider than you are, but you can definitely borrow some big comfy PJs from me."

The sheriff gave me a grin. "Will there be face masks and pillow fights?"

"What is with men and the slumber party jokes?" I asked as I put my hand on his forearm. "Thank you, Sheriff."

He walked us out into the lobby, and I lingered back for a moment. "Tuck, I know you probably can't or won't tell me anything, but just for the sake of Cynthia, I wanted to ask. Are you any closer to catching the murderer? I mean, it doesn't seem like this theft and the murder are related, right?"

The sheriff made a very pronounced movement to the right with his eyes, and I glanced over to see Deputy Dillard watching us intently, a fact that the sheriff apparently wanted me to note.

"I'll take that as a 'No Comment' then," I said with a smile. "Guess I'll just have to figure out the answers myself then?"

"Harvey Beckett—" but I was already out the door before he could finish his sentence.

CYNTHIA SPENT the rest of the afternoon in a chair with Mayhem and Taco at her feet. I was never going to be a "pets are people" kind of person, but I definitely knew that they understood people, especially people who needed comfort. Rocky kept our guest supplied with hot chocolate, and I checked in with her every once in a while just to see that she had all she needed with her cocoa and her romance novel. Clearly she was fine because she barely broke her eyes from the page to smile at me when I passed.

Mart sent me text updates on Ariel's move regularly, and at about six, Cate and Lucas came in. "Mart mentioned that Cynthia was here and would be coming to dinner," Cate said. "I don't want her to worry about seeing me or anything, so I thought I'd stop by. Let her know it's okay."

I hugged her and said, "Thank you" before pointing her over to the chair where Cynthia had ensconced herself.

I really wanted to hear that conversation, but I miraculously minded my own business and went about tidying the store and preparing the cash register drawer so we could leave right at seven. After all the drama today, pizza, friends, and celebration sounded so great.

A little before I closed, Cynthia and Cate returned to the front of the store, and Lucas got up from his chair in the café, where he'd been reading *A Man Called Ove*, which I'd handed him when it looked like Cynthia and Cate might be talking for a while. While I rang up the book with my friends and family discount, Cynthia and Cate kept talking, and I could tell just from the casualness of their conversation that all was well.

"We're going to go ahead and take Cynthia with us, if that's okay with you, Harvey? Figured she could maybe use a little wine to shake off this day."

Cynthia smiled and held up her book. "Plus, I just finished this. I never would have thought I'd like it, but it's so funny." *Bridget Jones's Diary* had won over another reader.

"She's been trying to get me to read that for weeks. I've been refusing because it seems ridiculous, but maybe I'll have to give it a shot," Cate winked at me.

"I'll see you guys in a bit. Don't eat all the Hawaiian pizza."

After they left, I spent the next few minutes reshelving the few remaining books and helping Rocky clean up in the café. Friday nights in this small town bookstore were pretty quiet.

At seven on the dot, Rocky and I locked up, and she headed out for date night with Marcus. He'd spent the afternoon helping Ariel move, and I expected he was ready to spend some time with his girlfriend and not with a bunch of middle-agers who would be in bed by ten p.m. at the very latest. I imagined Ariel and Cynthia felt the same, or maybe, I wondered, they would enjoy being with people who didn't feel the pressure to seem lively and busy. When I was their age, the weight of social expectation felt so heavy. Now, I couldn't care less. If I wanted to spend Friday night eating pizza and drinking wine with friends in a one-bedroom apartment, I would. Tomorrow night, I'd be up for TV and popcorn at home with my guy. That was all the social influencing I needed to do.

Daniel had brought my truck by on his way to Ariel's earlier, stopping in to tell me it was parked on the street, a gift I was especially grateful for since I really didn't want to make the walk home or ask him to come back into town to get me.

Mayhem jumped right in the truck, and Taco graciously lifted his front end so I only had to heft his rear up. Then, they went directly to their crates. I, however, had to climb awkwardly into the bed, a feat that could not by any means be described as graceful, and shut the kennel doors. Fortunately, a long day of sleeping had worn the pups out because they were each curled up inside their respective boxes by the time I closed them in. Thank goodness they weren't puppies. That would have been a fiasco.

I took a moment to load Ariel's new address on my phone and texted Daniel to say, "Be there in fifteen," and then headed out of town on Route 13 going North. The streetlights of St. Marin's ended in just a few blocks, and soon I was in the dark night of an

Eastern Shore evening. Light pollution was almost nonexistent here, and I rolled down my window and enjoyed the breeze as I occasionally glanced up at the stars above me.

I was a couple of miles outside of the town limits when blue lights came on behind me. My first thought was that Tuck was pranking me. He was notorious for his jokes on townsfolk, but when I saw Dillard step out of the patrol car, I decided it must be something else. I hoped no one was in trouble.

"Hey Harvey," he said. "Sorry to pull you over. But all your taillights are out."

"What?!" I said, opening the door and stepping out. "That's so weird."

I walked around to the back of the truck, and sure enough, not a light on in the rear of the vehicle despite the fact that my headlights were on.

"Well, that's odd. Gracious. I guess you can't see me at all from behind, huh?"

"Nope. Your truck's a lighter color, so that helps. But it's really not safe to drive like this. Especially out here. Someone might run right up on you." He held his flashlight onto the back of my truck.

"True. Well, I guess I can call Daniel. Have him come take a look. I don't suppose you want to just follow me in your car?" I was only half-joking. I could feel my relaxing evening disappearing.

"Why don't I just give you a ride to wherever you're going? We can pull the truck off the road and leave a note. I'll let the station know that it's out here. Then you and Daniel can come back in the morning and take a look. No reason to ruin your plans over this."

I hesitated. I didn't like the thought of leaving my truck here unattended, but I also didn't want to run Daniel all over creation after he'd spent the day lifting furniture. "Okay, but I have two dogs with me. Is it okay if they ride along?"

A shadow passed over Dillard's face, and for a second, I wondered if he disliked dogs or maybe was allergic. But then I remembered how he'd given Mayhem such good scratches. Maybe he didn't like the idea of hair in his patrol car.

"Um, sure. Let me put a blanket on the back seat."

"Cool. Thanks, Chad. I'll get them out." I repeated my awkward climb into the bed and nudged the two hounds awake and out into the bed, where I clipped on their leashes before helping them get down. Taco definitely needed to go on a diet.

Then, we walked over to Dillard's car, and I opened the back door. Normally, both of these dogs took to a ride like they had invented NASCAR, but tonight, they hesitated and went stiff-legged as I urged them in. Eventually, I had to lift both of them onto the backseat and quickly close the door.

I sat up front next to Dillard and thanked him again.

"No problem, Harvey. All part of the job."

He started the car and pulled back out on the road.

I glanced back at the dogs and found them both sitting bolt upright and staring into the front of the car. "Lay down, guys. It's not far, but you can still catch a quick nap." Neither of them moved.

"Probably nervous about the unfamiliar smells in here," Dillard said. "Not all my passengers are as polite as they are."

I forced a small smile but kept looking back at Mayhem. She had her eyes fastened on the back of Dillard's head. I felt the hairs on my arm stand up. Something was wrong.

My suspicion was quickly confirmed when, instead of turning left into the complex where Ariel's apartment was, he kept driving straight. Only then did I realize he'd never asked me for the address.

I TRIED to keep my cool, act like I didn't realize what was happening. "So how are you liking St. Marin's?"

His face moved into a crooked smile, and he said, "It's nice. I like the quiet, being able to get out onto the water."

As he talked, I adjusted myself in my seat as if I was trying to get comfortable when really I was trying to reach my cellphone in my back pocket. Why, oh why, had I worn my tightest jeans? "You fish?" I had to keep this conversation going, keep him a little distracted.

"Yeah. Grew up fishing trout, but I'm finding that the challenge of catching bass is even more fun. I like a challenge in my kill."

I felt my heart rate quicken and tried to work the phone up and out of my pocket without giving away what I was doing. Almost there. "I'm one of those people you don't want to fish with. I don't like to bait the hook or take the fish off. I'm mostly there for the casting."

"Huh, that surprises me. Seems like you like to get your fingers into everything." He shifted in his seat. "Why don't you just hand me that phone now?"

I looked over and saw that he had drawn his pistol and had it pointed at my side. "What phone?"

"The one in your back pocket . . . or do you need to use the bathroom?"

For one second I thought about lying and saying I just had to pee, but I decided against it. No need to make him angry.

I leaned forward and got the weight off my rear so I could hand him my phone. I tried to move slowly enough that my thumbprint would register and I could at least dial someone's number, but he snatched it from my hand before I could open the contacts.

"I do feel bad about this, Harvey. I want you to know that. But your snooping, well, the sheriff warned you that it could get you into trouble. You should have listened."

My mind was whizzing around, trying to figure out exactly what was going on, but I was clueless about everything except the fact that clearly Dillard had something to hide. "I actually did listen, Chad. I don't know what you heard, but I haven't been snooping at all except—"

Dillard snickered. "Except that you have at the behest of our beloved Tucker Mason. He had you looking into things that could have been better left unexplored."

I tried to read his expression from the corner of my eye. He looked calm, collected, which terrified me. But it did mean that he would probably talk, and if I'd learned one thing from TV shows it was that keeping the attacker talking was the victim's best bet. "I'm really confused, Chad. Surely you knew that the sheriff would eventually execute a warrant on the bank and figure out what was going on with the theft there."

"Eventually was the key word, but you kept pressing, kept asking questions, and he moved more quickly than I thought he would. I had hoped that the murder would keep him busy long enough that by the time he looked into what happened at the bank, we'd be long gone."

He had a partner, so maybe Cynthia had duped me. I shook my head slowly. "You really are going to have to help me here. I'm just not following." That statement was true, but I was beginning to formulate a theory. A little too late, though.

"You'll see soon enough." He turned onto a narrow gravel road, and I estimated that we were about ten minutes past Ariel's apartment. Too far from town for me to run and in entirely the wrong direction if anyone came looking for me on my expected route.

The road turned out to be a long, nearly abandoned driveway, and he parked his patrol car in front of a run-down cabin that seemed to sit right on the water. A screened in porch that was no longer a screen against much of anything faced the drive, and leaning against one of the pillars, I saw Renee Forsham. She was smiling, and I felt all the blood run out of my extremities.

"You know her?"

"Sure do. Known her all my life." Dillard smiled at me, then, and in that moment, I saw the resemblance. Forsham was his mother.

I decided not to blurt that out, though, because I figured maybe there was some advantage to seeming like I was missing things. But I was quickly putting the pieces together. The theft, the murder, Cynthia's involvement.

The one thing I didn't know yet was why. What exactly was going on to make this mother-son duo not only steal, but kill someone?

Dillard stepped out of the car, and, for one moment, I thought about running. But then I heard Mayhem snarl and Taco start his basset hound braying, and I knew that if I did that, the dogs would definitely be dead. I couldn't have that. I just couldn't.

So I stepped out of the car and waited. He gestured toward the house. "Those two will quiet down once they can't see you anymore, I expect."

I looked back at Mayhem and gave her a nod, hoping she knew what to do, and then I walked up the creaking steps to the porch.

"Nice to see you again, Harvey. Too bad you're going to miss the memorial service tomorrow." Her voice was calm, almost light, and I found bile rising in my throat, from anger or fear I wasn't sure.

Dillard gave me a shove toward the open door of the house, and I stepped into what was obviously a long-neglected vacation cabin. The old ship's wheel on the wall was covered in cobwebs, and the sofa looked like it had been an antique in the days of Archie Bunker. "Sit down," Dillard said, gesturing to the couch.

I dropped onto a cushion, and a cloud of dust rose up around me like I was Pigpen. I feigned a coughing fit to give myself a few seconds to study the room.

Forsham and Dillard sat down on folding chairs across from me and started playing cards on a round, wooden table. Poker, maybe. I'm not much of a card player, but there was a lot of bidding going on. They were only playing with fun-size candy bars, but it looked to me like they were seasoned players given the quickness of the game and their relatively high bids.

I wasn't sure what was going on here, but as my captors were largely ignoring me, I decided not to rock the boat. I looked around the room as surreptitiously as I could, hoping I'd see an easy exit. But while there was another door at the other end of the room by the kitchen, I didn't think I could make it there before Dillard could draw his gun. Besides, the dogs were still trapped in the car, and they needed me to save them.

I spotted a set of fireplace tools by the woodstove just to my left and thought I might be able to grab one and disarm Dillard before Forsham could get to me. But then I wasn't sure I could fight her off. She was older than I was, but she looked strong.

I kept scouring the room, hoping to see my magic escape ticket. A giant bowl of acid I could grab and toss on both of them long enough for me to get free and release the dogs. A rickety support beam I could kick out to drop the ceiling on just the two of them. A length of rope I could fasten into a lasso to drag them off their feet. Despite the fact that I found nothing of this sort, the hope kept me distracted and away from panic. I needed to keep my wits about me, that I knew.

After a dozen hands or so, Dillard had lost all of his candy to Forsham. "See, this is why you get in trouble, Chad. You bet too high and get caught up in the stakes. You have to be smarter with your bids."

Dillard rolled his eyes and sniffed. "Mom," he sounded like a petulant teenager, "you know that this isn't my fault. Those men swindled me."

His mother frowned. "Chad, you must take responsibility for your part in all this. You know that?"

I felt strangely awkward watching this mother-son moment. It felt like I was seeing a young boy scolded by his mommy for the fact that he'd kicked a ball into someone's window. But, of course, this was a full-grown man, a police officer at that.

Dillard sighed. "I did take responsibility. See? She's right there." They both turned to me, and I wanted to crawl back into the cushions of the dusty couch.

I took the chance to ask one of the seventy-five million questions swimming through my head. "You think adding kidnapping to your list of crimes is a good idea, Chad?" I wasn't sure what I hoped would happen with this line of talk, but I just kept going. "I mean, if you do get caught, is it wise to have another felony for the judge to consider?"

Renee ignored me completely. "You did, honey. That's good. But how are we going to handle this? We can't let the sheriff solve these cases, not yet. Not until next week. You know that."

Forsham's tone was patient, like a teacher talking to a problem student.

"I do know that, Mom." Dillard stood up, and his chair fell back against the floor. "I have a plan."

"Okay, then let's hear it."

I wasn't particularly eager to hear Dillard's plan for killing me, but I didn't have much choice.

"I'm going to take her out into the woods and use that shotgun." He pointed to a long barrel that I hadn't noticed behind him by the table. "Then, I'll take her back to near her truck and leave her. When I puncture the tire, it'll look like she wandered off into the woods and got shot by a hunter."

I started to speak up and point out that deer season was in the fall so no one would fall for that but Forsham spoke before I did.

"Good plan. Right in the midst of spring turkey season. Plus, she headed out about dusk when the birds were likely to be moving. One question though, what about the dogs?" She sounded almost proud of her murdering son.

"Oh, I'll shoot them, too. Make it look like a hunter was covering his tracks."

I whimpered. I didn't want to die, but the idea of Mayhem and Taco being shot was too much for me. "You don't have to kill me, you know. I really don't know anything. Even now."

Forsham peered at me. "Well, you know that Chad and I are related, don't you? And you know I stole that money from the co-op and blackmailed Cynthia."

I shook my head. "I don't know any of that."

Renee stood up and walked toward me. "Okay, I do know that," I tried to sound calm and reasonable, "but the sheriff already knows, too. I mean, you could just leave me here, tie me and the dogs up or something, and get out of town. If all you need to do is get to next week, then you don't have to add murder to your crimes. Just leave me here." I didn't relish the thought of being tied up in this depressing place, but at least I'd be alive and so would the dogs.

"I'm afraid that just won't work," Renee said. "See, the sheriff has put a freeze on my accounts. So I can't help Chad out of his mess. The only way I can do that is through my sister's money."

I really have to learn to think before I speak. "But she didn't leave you much?"

Renee glared at me, and I cowered back against the dusty couch. "She did leave her young nephew a fair sum, though." The bitterness in her voice could have cut flesh. "But to claim our inheritance, I need to be at the memorial playing the grieving sibling. Nope, we can't run. Not yet. Not until I get the check from the lawyer."

The picture was coming together more fully now, and fortunately, my natural curiosity kept me asking questions. The longer they talked, the longer I had to figure my way out. "Chad's mess? You mixed up in something?"

Dillard's face snapped toward mine and then back to his mother's. "I told you, they scammed me."

"Scammed you, my foot. You lost that hundred thousand by betting on the wrong team, son. No scam there. Just bad judgment. Now, you can't pay, and they're going to take their payment out of your knees." Her voice had lost even the little warmth it had before. "You have a gambling problem."

Chad groaned. "It's not a problem, Mom, just bad judgment, like you said." He was pleading.

Forsham softened visibly. "It's okay, honey. Mama's going to fix it again, and then we'll start over." She pulled her son into her chest and caressed his head. "But first, we have to fix this problem here."

"Wait, what about the sheriff? Doesn't he know that you killed Wilma? What good is it to kill me if he already knows what's going on?" I was grasping at straws here, hoping that I had it right.

"Oh, he hasn't figure that out yet. But he will. By then, though, we'll be gone." Forsham sounded so sure of herself. "He doesn't know the connection between Chad and me, but that's not long coming. Now that he knows about the bank money, he'll start digging. Probably already has."

"You don't think he'll put it all together this weekend?" I asked with dwindling hope.

"Honey, you know as well as I do that even law enforcement takes a break on weekends. There's no way he can pull my records until Monday. I meet with the lawyer on Monday morning. Gullible man believed the story that I had a sick cat to get back to, and then, I'll be out of town, and Chad will, too. We just need two more days."

I tried begging again. "I can give you two more days. Please just leave us here."

"Too risky," Dillard said. "Get up."

I made myself limp like I'd seen toddlers do and tried to become dead weight. But he was strong and just picked me up over one shoulder and marched me toward the front door.

As we reached the porch, I could hear Mayhem and Taco barking for all they were worth, and I said a silent word of thanks to them for their loyalty. Then, I let out the loudest scream I could and kicked with all my might.

I must have surprised Dillard because he dropped me, and I ran as fast as I could to the patrol car and grabbed one of the back doors. Mayhem and Taco leaped out like lightning bolts and charged at Dillard, who had fortunately dropped the shotgun when he dropped me.

Still, I lunged after them, hoping to grab their trailing leashes before he could get to the gun. But I was too late. He already had the shotgun in his hands and was raising it to his shoulder.

Just then, I heard tires on the driveway gravel and turned back to see blue lights speeding up the lane followed by a caravan of cars including Daniel's green pick-up truck. Sheriff Mason slammed the car to a halt next to me, and Daniel's truck whizzed right by, clipping Dillard in the leg just as he fired a shot at the dogs. Dillard cried out, and the shot went high.

As the sheriff jogged up toward the house, he shouted, "You okay?" in my direction and looked at me just long enough to see me nod before he ran to Dillard and handcuffed him.

"Daniel, Renee Forsham. Back door," I shouted from my prone position on the ground, two dog leashes firmly clasped in my extended hand.

He didn't hesitate and was off with the sheriff close behind him as my dad came and put a foot square in the middle of Dillard's back. "Don't even think about it," Dad said. I wondered how long he'd wanted to say that.

At that moment, I heard a shot, then a loud shout from the back of the house. I scrambled to my feet and would have run to Daniel if Bear hadn't grabbed my arms and held me in place. "Just wait, Harvey," he said softly, but firmly, in my ear.

For a few more excruciating seconds, I strained against his grip until I saw Daniel walk around the house with Renee Forsham thrown over his shoulder like a sack of potatoes. Then, I slumped back against Bear and felt Henri lay her face against my shoulder. "He's okay," she said as if both to convince me and to be sure herself.

Daniel walked with Renee to the sheriff, who was just coming back off the screened-in porch and held onto her while the sheriff put her handcuffs. Then, Dad let Dillard up and walked him to the sheriff's patrol car where he and his mother were both put in the backseat.

I stared at Daniel a long minute and then the dogs and I finally sprinted to him, jumbling into a mass of paws and arms that brought us all to a heap on the ground.

After I got a good look at him when Stephen and Walter took control of the dogs, I could see he was fine. "The shot?"

"I'm not sure if she was aiming at me or just trying to scare me, but there's a pine back there missing some bark about twenty feet in the air." He gave a rough laugh and helped me to my feet.

"You okay?" he asked as he looked at me closely.

"I am." I leaned into his chest. "But I almost wasn't."

He squeezed me tight, and I leaned hard into him as the tears began to fall.

11

---

*O*nly after the sheriff pulled out with Dillard and Forsham in his car did I notice that most of my friends were there. Mom and Dad, Lu, Stephen and Walter, Henri and Bear, Pickle, Cate and Lucas, Woody, Mart, Elle, even Ariel and Cynthia. It looked like even Pickle had canceled his weekly date with his wife to come help Ariel. I felt a little embarrassed that everyone had needed to come help me, too. They'd all come to my rescue, and just the sight of them set loose my tears again.

Daniel walked me to the bed of his truck and helped me up so I could sit there while Woody, who apparently was also a part-time paramedic, could look me over. "How did you all find me?" I asked the semi-circle of people I loved who had formed around me.

"Good thing Taco likes to eat," Pickle said as a tiny, black woman next to him laughed.

"Wait, are you Mrs. Pickle?"

The woman doubled over. "Why, yes. Yes, I am. Matilda." She put out a hand. "Nice to meet you, Harvey."

I leaned over and shook her hand, admiring the many rings as I did. "Oh, it's so nice to meet you finally. Sorry for all the excitement."

"Are you kidding? This is a huge step up from wings!" Pickle squeezed her close.

I smiled and then looked at Daniel, "What's this about Taco's appetite?"

He shrugged. "When he was a puppy, he'd take off all the time, following Lu's truck. So I got him a GPS tracking chip for his collar." He bent down and picked up the portly pup to show me the blue chip by his ID tag. "When you didn't show at Ariel's apartment, we started to get worried. I knew you'd have the dogs with you, so I just checked out Taco's location on my phone. You were way out here, and I knew that wasn't right. There's nothing out here."

Woody stepped back from checking my eyes with the penlight he always had in his chest pocket and said, "So we all loaded up and headed out. Tuck called the station to ask Dillard to come out, too, but Harriet told him that Dillard hadn't been in all night."

Lu jumped up onto the tailgate next to me. "Tuck had been suspicious of Dillard ever since that incident with Cynthia." She smiled at the young woman standing by the side of the truck.

"So that's why he came in lights going and dust flying." Mart said as she pushed her way onto the tailgate next to me. "She okay?" she asked Woody.

"Yep. She's fine."

"I told you," I said. "They didn't even tie me up."

"Why in the world didn't you run then, Knucklehead?" Cate said.

Stephen, Walter, and Mart all said at the same time. "The dogs."

I smiled, and Cate rolled her eyes.

"You know you'd do the same for Sasquatch," I said.

She looked back at her car, and I could see a pair of shiny black eyes watching from the front seat. She shrugged. "Probably."

If Mom and Mart had gotten their way, I would have been shuffled off to bed immediately, but I was still shot through with adrenaline. More, I was still craving pizza, white pizza with extra garlic.

So most of us caravanned our way back to Ariel's while Dad and Daniel went to get my truck. I ate two pieces of white pizza and two cupcakes in the time it took them to get back, so when they returned, I was a little less shaky.

"The wiring for your lights had been pulled. All fixed," Daniel said with a small smile that quickly turned into a grimace. "He did nick the paint when he popped the lenses off."

At that point, all the decorum I'd been trying to keep in place fell aside, and I let loose a tirade of swear words that made me feel much better. Even Mom, the prim and proper lady she was, applauded my outburst.

Mart then got me a cup of hot tea and a third cupcake, and I sat down on Ariel's very comfy used sofa and let the adrenaline leave my body.

"So Forsham is Dillard's mom?" Cynthia looked appalled.

"I know. That's a little creepy what with the love notes and things on those flowers," Marcus said.

"I've been thinking about that," I said. "I think she intended for you to think they were from Dillard, not from her."

Cynthia sighed. "That's less weird, but no less creepy." She leaned her head on Ariel's shoulder.

"So any idea why?" Cate asked as she picked up my feet and began to rub them.

"I'm not totally sure." I slid down on the couch. "But I think it may have something to do with gambling." I described their weird game of poker and their conversation. "So maybe he was in debt and needed the money or something."

At that moment, Sheriff Mason came in and, hearing me, said, "That was it. Dillard was in way over his head with some unsavory folks from Atlantic City. Seems he has a bit of a gambling problem."

"Oof," Lucas said. "Gambling addiction is some serious stuff. My roommate in college battled that a long time."

Tuck nodded. "He probably didn't murder anyone, though. Right?"

Lucas shook his head. "Not that I know of."

"Addiction is an illness. Murder, not so much," Lu said.

"I'm still confused, though," Mom said with her arms stretched over her head like she was reaching for the explanation up in the ceiling fan. "Why murder Wilma Painter?"

"Oh, that one's easy. She figured out what was going," Ariel said. "Right? She was going to turn them in?"

The sheriff opened a beer and then sat down on the floor between Lu and Henri. "Yes, but not only that, apparently, Wilma and Renee had been rivals for a long time. Believe it or not, Renee was jealous of Wilma's life here, small and somewhat unhappy as it seemed to be. So when Wilma said she was going to come to me about this scam Renee had concocted to pay off

Chad's gambling debt, Renee convinced Chad that the only recourse was to kill her."

"He killed her or she did?" Rocky asked.

"She ended up doing it. Dillard refused. Some code of honor as a police officer or something." Tuck shook his head. "But he didn't hesitate to cover it up, so not much honor there."

I let out a hard laugh. "The funny thing was they thought I had all this figured out and was going to expose them before they could take their money and run. But I had no clue. If they hadn't kidnapped me tonight, they probably wouldn't have gotten away with it."

"Thank God for small blessings," Mart said with a wink.

"Always a silver lining," Cate chimed in.

"A glass half full," Stephen added.

I rolled my eyes. "You guys sure know how to cheer a woman up." I stood. "Now, can someone kindly drive me and my dog home. I'm not sure I trust myself behind the wheel."

THE NEXT MORNING, the crowd that gathered for Wilma's memorial service was substantial. Marcus had offered to cover the store for me so I could go. I wanted to pay my respects.

Surprisingly, it turned out that she had been equally kind to most of the people in town, giving extensions on loans and offering great interest rates for most of the businesses on Main Street. Even Henri was seeing the way Wilma dressed her down in a new light. "She warned us. Not everyone would have done that."

As one person after another stood to praise Wilma or to tell stories about her temper and sullen attitude, I thought of how kind she had been to Cynthia about the theft, and it made me wonder if she had known about Ariel's living arrangement all along. I suspected she had and had just let it be.

After the service, my friends and I gathered to do what you do when remembering someone who has died. We spoke of her kindly and wished goodness on her in the next part of her journey. Then, we decided to go get lunch. None of us felt like going to the potluck lunch in the church's Fellowship Hall. It was a little too much to make conversation just now.

We headed toward Lu's food truck, which was parked a tasteful distance up the street from the funeral, to provide sustenance without being predatory. Lu was a wise business woman.

"Wilma loved the chicken mole," Lu said as she handed me my two tacos. "Every Thursday, that was her lunch." I smiled at the image of Wilma eating from a food truck. Those little things, they remind me that no matter what a person may seem on the outside, they always have more to show.

Tuck joined us for lunch and let us know that both Forsham and Dillard had been charged with theft, and Forsham was also being charged with murder, with Dillard as an accessory. Their confessions, given in the hopes of gaining leniency, would make the process of justice swift and clear.

I was relieved, but also sad. Jealousy. Addiction. They had stolen so much in that family. It broke my heart a little.

BACK AT THE shop that afternoon, Stephen and Walter came in with Ollie following behind, a large canvas in his hands. "We want to show you something, Harvey," Stephen said. "Let's go in there." He gestured to the café.

I lifted my chin and looked at him from beneath my narrowed eyes. "What's going on?"

"Just want you to see this, okay?" He put a hand on the small of my back and steered me to a table in front of the window. "Sit."

I glanced at Rocky, and she shrugged before coming around to stand beside me.

Ollie set the sheet-covered canvas in front of me. "I hope you like it," he said quietly before pulling the sheet off.

There, in the most amazing array of blues, greens, and silvers I had ever seen was my face. It was a portrait of me, wild, graying hair, green eyes, blue glasses, and a massive armload of white peonies in my arms. All crafted from folded pages of books.

I clamped my hand to my mouth and gasped. "That's me," I finally said.

Ollie looked at me with his eyebrows high on his forehead. "Do you like it?"

"Are you kidding?" I stood up and hugged him. "I have never loved a piece of art so much in my life."

"And that's saying something," Stephen added, "because she never likes pictures of herself."

"Ollie, it is amazing. But why me?"

"You're a kind person, Harvey. To everyone. Always. Even to people who you think have done horrible things, you ask why, instead of just writing them off. I wanted to capture that." Ollie seemed a little embarrassed by his own eloquence.

Still, now I was really crying. The kindness in those words stole my breath.

"But the other reason was because Daniel asked me to paint you.

He commissioned this piece." Ollie looked over my shoulder, and there, on the sidewalk, Daniel was smiling.

I raced outside and hugged him.

"I think he got you. I think he got you perfectly," he said and kissed me.

PLOTTED FOR MURDER

BOOK 4 IN THE ST. MARIN'S COZY MYSTERY SERIES

*W*hen Mart dismissed my idea of covering All Booked Up's Harvest Festival float with entirely pumpkin-themed book covers, I knew she was probably right. But it wasn't until I realized that I'd need to scan and then print approximately 80 bazillion covers and then pay to have them blown up to a size that people could actually see from the side of the road that I gave in. As much as I wanted to both introduce people to great titles like *How Many Seeds in a Pumpkin?* and *Pumpkin It Up!*, my favorite cookbook of the season, I wasn't up for that much investment in time or money.

Besides, Mart's idea was much better. Cate, our friend and artist, had already made the huge pumpkin for the center of the float, and everyone had their costumes all set. The only thing left was to convince Taco that the treats would come to him if he just sat on that doghouse by the typewriter. The problem was, Taco wasn't much interested in being Snoopy. Still, I knew we'd make our Great Pumpkin float work, especially since my boyfriend Daniel had agreed to be Charlie Brown, bald cap and all. Mart was going to be Lucy, of course. She had the attitude and the black hair after all, and I knew my best friend could be as disdainful as the part required.

I was going to be Peppermint Patty, despite Mart's protests that I should be Lucy since clearly Daniel fawned over me like the football-missing Charlie mooned over Lucy. But I had been Peppermint Patty's biggest fan since my seventh birthday when I realized she was the smartest and the most laid-back of all the Peanuts. Plus, I sort of already had the hair for it.

This was going to be our first year for the bookstore to have a float in the parade, and I was determined it would be win the competition. I wanted those bragging rights, and the trophy would look great in the shop's front window.

But I knew we had stiff competition. Our friend Elle Heron, who ran the local farm stand and a cut flower business, had taken the title for the past two years with her Rose Parade-inspired floats made entirely from autumn blossoms, and despite Cate's willingness to help with our float, I knew the art co-op's creation would be stellar what with all the painters and sculptors involved. Then, when you factored in the Maritime Museum's tall ship made in exactly the same fashion as an actual cutter and the sheriff department's whimsical and totally overblown HeeHaw theme, with our African American sheriff dressed as Minnie Pearl, we had to bring our best game.

Good thing my hound dog Mayhem loved to wear costumes because she was our piece de resistance as Woodstock, and I knew the crowd would love our friend Woody as Pigpen. He was creating his costume by doing a lot of sanding that day and not showering.

We had five days to finish our float, and I was determined it was going to be amazing. Well, it was going to be amazing if I could actually manage to apply this red paint without streaks. I hated painting, but Snoopy's doghouse was the last big prop for the float. Everyone else had done their part – Woody built the doghouse, Cate did that "great" pumpkin, Daniel had made that mechanical football to fly over his own head again and again. The least I could do was paint.

Just as I was doing the final trimwork around the opening for Taco's very soft dogbed, a necessity if we wanted him to actually make the ride, when Daniel showed up with what smelled very much like a breakfast burrito from Luisa Tucker's food truck.

I looked up only to see the burrito waving like a mirage in front of my eyes. It was 8am, and besides Mrs. Chevalier's cinnamon rolls, nothing was better than Lu's burritos. They were cheesy and spicy and filled with the best eggs and sausage I had ever tasted, and that's saying something because I'm a southern woman and I know my eggs and sausage. "You sure know the way to my heart, Daniel Galena," I said as I reached up and snatched the burrito from his hand.

"I sure hope so," he said as he bent and kissed the top of my head. "But if all it took was a burrito, I would have started there." He winked as he sat down on a paint bucket next to me. "Looks good." He nodded toward the doghouse as he ate half a burrito in one bite.

"You think so? I feel like it's pretty sloppy." I eyed the streaks I could still see in the bright red paint.

"It does. Plus, it'll be far away. It doesn't need to be perfect."

I dropped the brush. "That settles it, then. I'm going to silence the 10% of me that is perfectionistic and let the 'good enough' 90% hold sway. I declare this dog house complete." With that, I tucked into my burrito with force.

After I had inhaled that cheesy goodness, I looked at Daniel. "So what brings you by besides the promise of the sheer joy on my face when you handed me Lu's food?" Daniel and I were together most days, but he wasn't exactly what you'd call a morning person. Most days, he and Taco came by just as I opened at 10, headed to his mechanic's shop up Main Street.

"Taco was lonely." He pointed over to where he had tied up his basset hound next to Mayhem on the bike rack at the backside of the alley near an open field.

I grinned. "Oh, Taco was, was he?"

"He was. He misses his girl when he doesn't get to see her for a couple of days."

"Oh yeah? Well, I'm glad you brought him by then."

"How was Mart's race anyway?" Daniel reached into his backpack and produced two more burritos, and my heart skipped a beat.

I kissed him on the cheek as I grabbed my second full meal and said, "It was good. Kind of fun to be back on the West Coast again."

Mart was a runner. It was a part of our friendship that would never align. I ran only under threat, and Mart ran half-marathons once a month and full marathons a couple times of year. We had long ago agreed to not try to understand the other's running perspectives. But I went to every race I could, and when she said she was going to run the Humboldt Redwoods Marathon in Northern California, I immediately signed on as her roadie.

It had been more than a year since I'd been back in northern California, the place Mart and I had lived before coming back to my home here on the Eastern Shore of Maryland, and I was eager to visit the eucalyptus forests again. I missed their smell, and I ached for the Pacific Coast with it's cliffs that looked out over the ocean and lines of pelicans diving into the surf. Plus, Humboldt County was perfect. All evergreen forests and pretty lakes plus just enough town in Eureka to find really good food, even better wine, and some good music, too. As soon as Mart had signed up, we'd decided to make it a long weekend out there.

We'd been gone since last Wednesday, and while I'd had a blast – including wearing a ridiculous hat with faux fur and dangling bead trim to cheer Mart on as she took first in her age group in the race – I was glad to be back home to St. Marin's. And to Daniel. I'd missed him.

"She rocked it. I think she could have run another 26.4 miles if she'd been allowed. But by the time she was done, she was starving. You know my favorite meal is breakfast, so we hit this place called The Chalet House of Omelettes."

"Cheddar and mushrooms?"

Oh, he knew me so well. "You know it. But the spectacular part was watching Mart eat two omelets and a short stack of pancakes. For a tiny woman, she can really put it away." I did not miss the irony of the fact that I had just shoved a second, full-size burrito into my mouth while I made this statement, but I didn't care. Lu's burritos were that good.

"Did you make it down to the city?" Daniel looked over at the dogs as he asked.

"Just on the way to and from SFO, the airport, I mean." I leaned over so he could look me in the face. "We didn't see anyone. I did, however, force Mart to take me for take-out at Burma Superstar since it wasn't out of the way on our trip over the Golden Gate. I *needed* a tofu tower and those deep friend string beans." I tried to make my answer seem light and fun, but I knew there was a lot riding on my answer.

"Oh, okay. I wasn't sure if you were going to spend more time there."

"Nope. I love that city, but I didn't have anyone I wanted to see there." I wiped the paint off my hands and then pulled a bucket up next to him. "You are the only man I want in my life. And I didn't even want that guy when I had him. You don't need to worry."

I had been married when I lived in San Francisco, but that marriage was broken in some fundamental ways, mainly the husband in that marriage was broken, so it had ended before I moved back east. But I knew that the fact that I'd been married before was a tender spot with this sweet man I loved.

"The only love I have in San Francisco is that tofu tower. Okay, and maybe the omelets at Louis'. Oh, and the pork rolls from . . . "

He kissed me and then said, "Okay, so my main competition is food. I can work with that."

"As long as you bring me burritos every so often, we shouldn't have a problem," I said slyly as I pushed myself to my feet. How come the ground got lower every time I sat near her? "You're early for the shop. Want to come in?" I pointed toward the back door of the shop.

"Sure," he stood easily from his own paint bucket, and I gave him the evil eye. "How can I help?"

Those four words offered so easily. Oh, they made my heart sputter. "Well, now that you've asked . . . "

While I put the paint away, he got Taco and Mayhem and brought them behind us into the bookstore. They immediately headed to the big orthopedic beds I'd placed in the front window. They were a gift from our favorite customer Galen had got them through an Instagram deal he was offered by a dog company. They had hired his bulldog Mack as their spokesdog, and now Mack was flush with merch and ready to share. Plus, dogs in the window were always good for tourist traffic, especially if a bulldog with a pronounced underbite joined them. During the summer high season, those pups had been all the pr I needed for the store.

Daniel had just brought out the last of the pumpkin books I needed for the new window display when Mart burst through the front door. She was sweaty and out of breath, something she hadn't been even at the end of this weekend's marathon.

"Call Tuck. There's been a murder."

"What?! Mart slow down," I said even as I grabbed my phone from the counter by the register. "Who's dead?

"Coach Cagle. I just found his body on the high school track."

To Read More of *Plotted For Murder,* **pre-order your copy here** - https://books2read.com/plottedformurder

HARVEY AND MARCUS'S BOOK RECOMMENDATIONS

Here, you will find all the books and authors recommended in *Bound To Execute* to add to your never-ending to-read-list!

- *Crime And Punishment* by Fyodor Dostoevsky
- *The Round House* by Louise Erdrich
- *The Night Watchman* by Louise Erdrich
- *The Myth of Solid Ground* by David L. Ulin
- *The Rest Of Us Just Live Here* by Patrick Ness
- *Why Didn't They Teach Me This In School* by Cary Siegel
- *Crazy Rich Asians* by Kevin Kwan
- *The Best Bass Flies* by Jay Zimmerman
- *The City We Became* by N.K. Jemisin
- *Poison In Paddington* by Samantha Silver
- *I Capture The Castle* by Dodie Smith
- *Bruno, Chief Of Police* by Martin Walker
- *Operating Instructions* by Anne Lamott
- *Confederates in the Attic* by Tony Horwitz
- *Outlander* by Diana Gabaldon
- *Everything, Everything* by Michelle Yoon
- *Turtles All The Way Down* by John Green
- *Reading People* by Anne Bogel

- *The Goldfinch* by Donna Tartt
- *Master of the Mountain* by Henry Wiencek
- *In the Market for Love* by Megan Squires
- *A Man Called Ove* by Fredrik Backman
- *Bridget Jones' Diary* by Helen Fielding

I have personally read each of these titles and recommend them highly. See this list plus the recommendations from the other books in the series here - https://books2read.com/rl/HarveyAndMarcusRecommend.

Feel free to drop me a line at acfbookens@andilit.com and let me know if you read any or have books you think I should read. Thanks!

Happy Reading,

ACF

WANT TO READ ABOUT HARVEY'S FIRST SLEUTHING EXPEDITION?

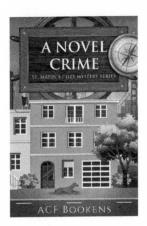

Join my Cozy Up email group for weekly book recs & a FREE copy of *A Novel Crime,* the prequel to the St. Marin's Cozy Mystery Series.

Sign-up here - https://bookens.andilit.com/CozyUp

ALSO BY ACF BOOKENS

St. Marin's Cozy Mystery Series

Publishable By Death

Entitled To Kill

Bound To Execute

Plotted For Murder

Tome To Tomb

Scripted To Slay

Proof Of Death

Stitches In Crime Series

Crossed By Death

Bobbins and Bodies

Hanged By A Thread

ABOUT THE AUTHOR

ACF Bookens lives in the Blue Ridge Mountains of Virginia, where the mountain tops remind her that life is a rugged beauty of a beast worthy of our attention. When she's not writing, she enjoys gardening with her son, cross-stitching while she binge-watches police procedurals, and reading everything she can get her hands on. Find her at bookens.andilit.com.

facebook.com/bookenscozymysteries

Made in the USA
Middletown, DE
13 May 2022

65585303R00125